Dreamwalker in Atlantis

"It's not about the words! This book is doorway into a history long forgotten.

We live in a world where so often books serve as nothing more than a reinforcement for our beliefs about the nature of reality and the history of consciousness on this planet. In other words, we want what we read to match our truth. Not for me. Instead books are passageways for a greater awareness, a vehicle to dive even deeper into Self and my own knowingness. 'Dreamwalker in Atlantis' did this for me. Not only did I find myself in the story of Yadar, I also found myself deep in my own experience of my lifetimes as a Dreamwalker in Atlantis.

For me, this book was not about the words on the paper, it was a portal into lifetimes and a civilization long forgotten despite its deep and unwavering impact on the world we live in today. And that's the best kind of book - one that serves as a gateway into deeper understanding of where we came from and what we are living today should the Atlantean Dream be of interest to you.

Thank you for a job well done, Erik Istrup! I highly recommend this book for anyone with an interest or connection between Atlantis and its relation to the story of Yeshua. You may just find yourself in your own Atlantean lifetimes remembering the intense beauty, splitting heartache and well, all of it."

~ Sar'h

Erik Istrup has also written
"Choose a simple living" (2014).

See also *The Adventures of Luzi Cane*:
The Soul of the White Dragon (2017)
Rider of the Crimson Dragon (2019)
Return of the Unicorn (2019)

Dreamwalker in Atlantis

by Erik Istrup

Contents

Preface

I chose to let the fictitious protagonist, Yadar, be the author, and most of the time let him describe places and things he experiences in his dreams and meditations, from the time in which he lived, which is around the end of the Atlantic Period about 14,000 years ago, Alt, as it was called at that time. Sometimes, however, I use the terms we use today to facilitate comprehension and to avoid long explanations. Seen from Yadar's perspective, he has infinite opportunities regarding choices he can make into his future. Since I, however, am the actual author, the experience line that goes from Yadar's time to mine is already experienced by a part of my soul's consciousness, and is, therefore, in terms of events, fixed.

Some people you will encounter in this story have names that do not fit with today's girls' and boys' names, but I used the names I sense the characters have.

Although Yadar is a fictional character, and you can read the novel as fiction, I use Yadar to describe things and experiences drawn from different incarnations or lives. You can say it is the same soul that has experienced these lives through different people. Some information is given by other awarenesses.

Some consciousnesses that appear as persons in Yadar's story are reborn and live today. If you are one of those, you may have a sense of recognition when you read about yourself.

Many of the lives have been about travel; about movement. Either as a pioneer to explore the new, or as a diplomat to bring balance and harmony in a world most often seen as chaotic and unfair. On a higher level, it has been about raising a hand saying "yes" when asked to volunteer for development work.

There is reference to a people, Shee, which we know as elves, but who name themselves Sidhe.

While working on the book, the events that I described touched me. Often so much that I had to pause and dry the tears or just go into the experience. But let's get started on the story.

- Erik Istrup

Introduction

Let me start by presenting myself. After that I will tell you why you can read this book. For now, you can call me Yadar. It may sound a bit cryptic, but you will soon get an explanation.

I have no biological family and live alone in a small apartment in the temple area. I am associated with a particular temple, but I also work in others, depending on where my expertise is needed. I have my private study in the temple and there are various service functions associated with it.

You must know that the book cannot be publicly available until its content cannot lead to people being hurt due to the knowledge it contains.

In this life, I am convinced that I have lived in the past, i.e., before I was born into this life, and also will come to live again after leaving this. That is why I am called Yadar in this life while in other lives I have other names and other personalities; yes, and different gender. Since I have only recently realised that I have lived in the past, I also write hoping others can see that this is how things work. Perhaps one of my souls' incarnations in the future could benefit from the book.

I'm a dreamwalker, but it's only one of my many chores. I will tell you more about this later, but a dreamwalker is a person who accompanies the consciousness of a person back toward its starting point, shortly before, during or after the body is dead. The place is called the Flower Bridge. From here, the consciousness continues on by itself.

I am also a researcher and work with all kinds of energy, dimensional shifting and life energy. As scientists, our work involves both exploring, and using our knowledge to help our fellow human beings in the widest sense. In the time I live, we are not so rigorous about whether it is work or interest that occupies our time. We usually do what we feel like doing and have the ability to do, and it is natural we share goods and favours. Here we do not keep accounts of who owes what, but more of who can use one's assets and who can contribute what you need. I am giving something to one person, but I receive a service from another. It is more about keeping the flow of services moving, rather than keeping track of whether I received enough in return from the one to whom I gave something. If I am in need of something, I can always find one who can help me.

During the period referred to here, we who are initiated can shift things slightly out of the third dimension toward the fourth, whereby temples and people become invisible and cannot be sensed by creatures in the third dimension. As I am one of the initiated, they have trained me in the deeper understanding of our world and its residents, and in various methods of gaining access to deeper layers of humanity's consciousness, and to affect them.

At this time, we do not have a concept of god, which, I understand, gets a lot of attention at a later stage in the planet's history. We are convinced that the source of life is in the physical body. Why should life energy be outside ourselves? It is the body that is alive, right? In addition, we research energy, in the form of vibration, sound and light. We use crystals in research, but I can understand, from my dreams, that the crystals will, over time, lose their power in later periods. The concept of god involves more than three dimensions, where the deity occupies the highest. I will come back to these metaphysical concepts later. The metaphysical concept, what lies beyond the physical world, is just beginning to emerge and is known only to a few here in the temples.

I will try to keep my story from my present chronological. On the other hand, it is extremely difficult, if not impossible, to put my journeys to other times in chronological order. Although I can sense a certain order, it is as if the level of consciousness of mankind fluctuates and is not simply increasing towards a higher development. Moreover, it is as if the individual dreams and visions are interconnected; not only with each other but also with what I experience while I'm awake. Later, I will go into more detail about the consciousness of mankind.

It is strange that in dreams I have prior knowledge that I do not have when I am awake. It is as if I jump into a life and link to the person's memory of what has gone before and to the people surrounding me. Sometimes I know the person I am facing from my waking state, even if the person looks different, has a different face or gender.

The work as a dreamwalker

It is morning and I am in my study in the temple. I have been out on the balcony placing crystals so the sunlight and the rain around noon will clear them, so they are ready for my work.

It is very unusual to have one's own study and a home on its own. People live in large groups, sleep together and work together. People do not feel the need to retreat and be by themselves. It is not in consciousness. We are about 100,000 people here in the temples, working more or less in secret on discovering our full awareness. We do so under the guise of looking for life energy, what makes a being able to live. It is an individual process to seek one's full awareness, but we share each other's experiences and try out different techniques. Unfortunately, we lost a boy the other day. He was working as a helper when he walked into a room where we were investigating the channels of consciousness using crystals.

I have many activities by which I contribute to the society and among these, as I said, is dream walking. That is precisely why Janir now visits me, announced by the service person, Cantor. I know Janir and her husband Jacor, but, true to say, I have recently been so absorbed in my work we have had no contact.

"Excuse me. I announce Janir's arrival. She wants to inform you of her errand herself."

"Thank you, Cantor. Just send her in.

"Dearest Janir. Come in, come in."

I flutter around a little, not sure in what order I must do the different things that a host should do.

Janir smiles. I catch her eyes and instantly feel relaxed.

"Thank you, Janir."

"And thank you, dear."

Janir is still smiling. She is an elderly woman. Much older than her face tells. Her eyes, however, cannot conceal her wisdom. Not that she tries to do so. She has mild features and radiates both gentleness and firmness, just like the planet she has always worked with. It is perhaps why today she wears a red dress reaching the floor. Embroidery almost covers it in dark red and brown shades, making it look like a topographic map of a desert area. Now I notice that the fabric in many places emits little flashes of light and I think of raindrops in the sunshine that irrigate the wilderness. If I wait a bit, the flowers will surely emerge from the red sand.

"Yes, it's beautiful, isn't it?"

"Well, yes. Sorry, I got lost in my own thoughts. It was something about desert sand, raindrops and flowers. Now I'll stay focused."

I fetch Janir a glass and pour water for both of us. We sit opposite each other.

While I'm trying to remember where we left, last we talked, Janir explains why she has come.

"Jacor has chosen to leave this world soon. We three have, frequently, discussed the topic and you know his arguments for not using the pyramid."

Yes, the arguments are familiar and we agree that it is incompatible with equality and humanity that only the elite can use the crystal bed in the pyramid to charge the body's cells with life energy and prolong life.

Janir continues, after taking a sip of water.

"Many oppose him, and even more think he is an old nitwit who makes a fool of himself. If they think he hurts the higher society's position, it will look bad, not only for him but also for his friends and family."

"He is stubborn, the dear Jacor, but how is he physically and mentally?"

"He's fine, but I sense fatigue. Or I should rather say that he's full up with this life. In particular, I see it in the way he moves."

"You come to ask me to be his dream walker companion?"

"Yes. There can be no question that you should be the one. I will also be with him."

"You know, Janir, that it will be a great honour for me to make this dream walk with Jacor. Have you thought when we can go into a little more detail about the event?"

"Come to us tomorrow, while the day is still young, and let us enjoy breakfast together."

"It's a deal. Say hello to Jacor and tell him I look forward to meeting him."

We get up, say our farewells and Janir floats out the doorway as if she does not touch the floor. I sense a faint scent of flowers and fragrant herbs; her characteristic fragrance.

I immediately note the appointment in my calendar, because I know from experience that I easily get distracted and forget even important arrangements.

Before I tell you more about the dream walk, you should hear about an experience I had the night before I was to meet Jacor and Janir.

The temple of rejuvenation

As I lie down for the night, I think with pleasure and expectation of the meeting tomorrow morning with Jacor and Janir. However, there is also a certain amount of sadness, because of Jacor's decision to leave, even though I feel I have accepted his decision.

I am expecting a fruitful meeting tomorrow and I ask for useful information about my work on energy and healing.

After some deep breaths, I slip into the layer between being awake and the real dream consciousness. The sound of the layer reaches me, but then I slip deeper down and soon I experience flying high above the sea and the clouds. There are holes between the clouds and I move downwards. The clouds part and I see a huge mountain of volcanic origin towards which I am heading. It appears like a huge red cone, but it is not erupting. There is snow on the top. Several smaller volcanoes surround it, also with snow on the top. The sun is shining on the side facing me, and, as I approach the place, I sense peace and harmony.

As I get closer, I see I am heading for the top. I feel I am moving too fast. If I follow my current course, I will hit close to the edge and blast straight into the rock side. There is a sensation of panic, but then I passed through the rock wall or a narrow opening. I did not see which. Now I am in a large, high-ceilinged space, almost like a temple, inside the mountain.

As I float up in the room and look around, I see a large opening where the light pours in. The room is very high in relation to the sea level and the icy wind blows into the room. My teeth rattle and the cold reaches into my innermost being. My whole body shakes.

"Where am I?" I say with chattering teeth, but get no answer. I study the details in the vast space. Further inside the cave, away from the opening, is a shield, and behind this a construction that does not make sense. There are people down there. I float closer.

For a moment, I find myself outside the mountain, out in the open and far up. This time there are no clouds, and the vast land I saw during my approach has become much smaller. I see the sea in the distance. Oh, *Hawaii*. I now recognise the mountain and sense I am far back in time. My past. Now I have the answer to where I am.

Suddenly I am back in the cave and become accustomed to seeing in the dim light. With chattering teeth, I try to get more details of the design.

On a kind of bed a human is lying on his back. Above the person is what seems like a lid. The top and bottom are identically crafted, oval and about one foot thick. The material looks like grey slate. The edges are rounded and the ovals are so large that even a large and tall person can lie stretched out.

I inspect the person on the couch. The man is lying on a white cloth. He is naked and must be awfully cold. There are several people around him, but

I can't see what they're doing. Something tells me that the man should receive healing. "Rejuvenation," I am being corrected.

The sound of an infant catches my attention and I see a woman with a child in her arms. A mother with her child, I guess. Why would someone bring a child up here in this cold? Mother and child are dressed in thick layers of clothes, but just breathing the cold and very thin air had to be terrible for the little one. Is the man dying, and are his wife and child there to support him and give him courage?

"The child is the one party in the event," I am told. "There is no family relationship between the man and the woman with her child."

"Are they taking the child's life force and giving it to the man?" I ask in horror. "That's terrible!"

"The child suffers no harm and the woman also benefits from the rejuvenation."

Thousands of questions are coming forth: "But what's going on? How does this system work? From where do they get the power, and how is the child connected to the man?"

"Magnetism, telepathy, cohesion."

My brain tries to find possible explanations of how the system works. My head is about to blow.

"Don't think, but feel what's happening!"

I try to relax, and after a short time I get some pictures I can take back to the awakened state to work with.

With a curiosity to stay, and an unspeakable desire to escape the horrible cold, I slide backwards out through the rock, into the open and back to the darkness in my dream state.

I am back to the dream's starting point and caught up in panic. "Wake up, wake up," I shout with my inner voice, and while I am battling to get up to the surface of the awakened state, I tumble, still half-asleep, to the table, where I have tools to write my experiences. I draw, write and think like a madman. I have to remember everything; I must lose nothing!

I lean back in the chair, exhausted, both in body and mind. Then I fetch the jug with water and a glass, pouring, spilling, and sit down again. The water helps, and I focus on its way into my body.

"The water is alive; the air is alive," I hear from a distance.

However, I can't make sense of the statement. I take some deep breaths, and then I return to the table and look at my sketches and notes.

It is madness to build the healing structure in such a terrible, inaccessible and hostile place! Is it to keep it away from the common people so that few can access the design?

Magnetism. The two plates, one above the man and the other under him, may contain magnets or be two large magnets. Telepathy. The child and the man must be telepathically connected to each other, but how can it help?

"A common expectation and the desire for rejuvenation, and that it must be done in harmony with everything; that is what you call nature or life."

"Cohesion? If the child and the man do not even share family ties, where is the cohesion?"

"The cohesion between the components of the child's body and the man's body."

"But the bodies did not even touch each other. How do I understand this cohesion?" I ask, even more perplexed.

"We'll give you a brief and accurate explanation, and you must accept even if you don't understand it all immediately. Be patient. It will come to you later."

I nod and place a blank piece of paper in front of me.

"No, don't use your mind. Close your eyes and see the pictures!"

"Yes!" I close my eyes and lean back in the chair. Waiting. Waiting. I get impatient. Where are the pictures? I sense into it, but realise I am not at all calm. I breathe deeply a few times and slip into a shallow sleep.

Shortly after, the pictures and a sense of knowing come to me. Only a few moments have passed since I shut my eyes, and now I am fresh and start to write.

"All the components of the human body come from the planet. All the building blocks of a child's body have come through the food that the child's mother has consumed, and the child's energy. All things on the planet have at one time or another been in touch with each other. This is where the cohesion comes from. The building blocks are familiar with each other and never forget this connection, even if they are far apart. At the lower or deeper level, this is the 'connection' between the child and the adult, and at a higher level it is the telepathic link. The mother has a natural connection with the child since she has recently been in contact with all the child's building blocks and has a profound telepathic connection to her offspring. Rejuvenation takes place because the child's new building blocks can, through cohesion, tell the man's old and worn building blocks what a new or healthy one looks like. The old building blocks have a kind of 'aha' experience and remember what they were like when they were new. They are, therefore, not a copy of the child's building blocks. Neither the child nor the mother nor the man share anything physically. The building blocks of the woman and man begin to repair or rebuild themselves. This requires special attention and patience as it will take time to rearrange things from the old to the new."

I feel dizzy after this.

"It's so simple! So simple! But what about the magnets?"

"The magnets bring the building blocks to vibrate in sync. Bring them to speak the same language at the same time. The low temperature is necessary to bring the building blocks down to a temperature at which they can go into resonance with the magnets. The inability of the magnetics to oscillate fast enough makes the siting of the construction in this cold environment necessary."

After this experience, I can see we have only remembered a snippet of our ancestors' knowledge. Now we work with what we do best, namely crystals, but it is not as effective, and the effects degrade relatively fast when it comes to regenerating the body.

Should I work with this method I experienced in dreams? That would be a magnificent achievement! I should most likely start right away, but the night is almost gone, and I must be able to do my best when I visit Jacor and Janir. I slip into a dreamless sleep.

Preparation for the dream walk

I feel refreshed after the morning bath and trot expectantly towards Jacor and Janir's dwelling. I wear my finest white cloth, adorned with a little gold embroidery at the edge, and new sandals. I shall meet with my dear friends and we shall prepare the dream walk with Jacor. I am impatient to tell them about my dream and feeling like a child who gets a long-awaited wish fulfilled.

This is a pleasant time of day. The coolness of the night has disappeared and the heat of the day has not yet arrived. A thought comes to me. Why do I find it so hard to tolerate the heat? I have lived in this climate all my life without ever getting used to it. It is not because I want to stay in a cool environment, but much of the day is too much for me and I only go outside if necessary. It has been like this my whole life. It is not something that has come with age.

I approach my destination. The side of the hedge towards the road is, as always, looking perfect, thanks to Janir. As I open the door, a small chime in the house signals to the residents that their guest has arrived. Jacor approaches me with a smile. With my errand in mind, my experiences with this dear friend whiz past my inner eye and I feel a warmth in the heart. So is he full of days?

Jacor greets me. "Yadar, dear friend, distracted as always!"

"Oh, I got lost in my own thoughts. I thought of all

I have experienced with you, and that's quite some, dear Jacor."

That could have been embarrassing. I must pull myself together and keep my thoughts in the present moment. We hug each other.

"Come, Janir is already sitting in the garden. We have a lot to talk about. Now that I reflect, it's a long time since we've had a proper talk, you and I. Am I right?"

Oh yes, I've been too busy with my many things. When will I learn?

It is as if Jacor reads my thoughts.

"Do not blame yourself and have a bad conscience. Living one's passion is just living while you're alive."

He slaps me gently on the back and shows me to the table beneath a large flamboyant tree. This lets the morning sun shine through the leaves, and the clusters of red flowers will also give us shade, especially when the heat sets in. They are always so thoughtful. Again, I get a bad conscience because I am always distracted in such situations where I must be a host. It bites itself in the tail. The less I want to be host, because I am distracted, the less exercise I get at being it, and thus I feel even less safe.

Janir gets up from the table and smiles.

"Welcome, dear Yadar. Where are your thoughts?"

"Oh, sorry, Janir. I was thinking of how distracted I

usually am and thus I was distracted. Sigh!"

"Cheers. I would call it thoughtfulness and even profundity, and that is positive, isn't it?"

"Take a piece of bread." Jacor hands the basket with fresh-baked bread towards me.

I smile and take a piece of bread that is still hot, touch it and smell it. Life is filled with gifts.

During the meal, we bring each other up to date with the larger things that have happened since we were last together. I don't have much to tell. It is as if it had all slipped from my memory after the dream last night. Everything else has become less important. I hear the couple's stories and make brief comments while I am waiting to tell about the great revelation I have received.

At last, I think the moment is appropriate, and Janir looks at me with a big smile.

"And what is it you are so impatient to tell?"

I feel embarrassed, but I am quick to forget it as soon as I start my story.

Both Janir and Jacor share my enthusiasm, but then Jacor frowns.

"Can't this lead to further divisiveness and perhaps give the power-holders even more power?"

"I haven't thought about that at all, only that everyone could enjoy the benefit of the discovery. I must consider this before I even start to write something. And I promise you, Jacor, that I will speak with you before I do anything at all."

I think of what Janir had told me the day before about Jacor's resistance to using the rejuvenation pyramid. I understand his comment.

"Thank you, I am happy to hear that."

I feel a little depressed, find a smile and slap my palms together.

"Let us forget my dream and concentrate on what I came to do … well in addition to visit you, that is."

The girl clears the table and leaves only water, fruit juice and fruit. Jacor tells about his desires in the context of the dream walk. It is not long before I have an overall picture of the landscape he has chosen to move through on his journey.

"Let's make an initial dream walk, where we go into the landscape you've described. You come with us, Janir," I say.

We shut off the outer senses and place ourselves in the chairs in the same order in which we will walk through the landscape, and take each other's hands. With eyes closed, focusing on an introductory picture, we find ourselves on a trimmed lawn with clusters of yellow flowers scattered around. Near us is a hedge, about three feet high, stretching to both sides as far as we can see. It has small bunches of tiny, white flowers. Right in front of us is an opening like an arch in the hedge, created from the hedge itself, and a narrow path of reddish sand going through the opening. We can't see what is on the other side, only the path that leads in there. We need to pass through the opening.

We walk next to each other, with Jacor in the middle, I to the left and Janir to his right. The arch becomes wider as we approach, so we can walk through side by side.

As we come through the opening in the hedge, the path goes down a hill. To the left a forest forms, at the outmost edge of which there is hazel. On the right are open spaces, with low mountains in the distance. Between the mountains and us is a wide river which bulges out in the middle to form a lake. There are swans on the lake's shiny surface. The sun shines from a blue sky with white clouds, and a gentle breeze brings the area's sounds and fragrances to us.

Jacor puts details in the landscape. Janir and I do not interfere. It is my job to keep us on the path we have already walked, so that, although Jacor's focus is out in the landscape, his centre is still between us on the path. Janir is Jacor's anchor.

As a dreamwalker, it is often my job to create the scenario that the client has to pass through, from a few hints and what else I know of the person. Although it is earthly things that dreamwalkers use in these scenarios, there must be nothing that can motivate the client to maintain contact with the Earth, such as food, drink and sex. We work with beauty in architecture and colours, grace and lightness, and the sense of freedom. I must interject here that I rarely make an initial dream walk with the client.

Where must the client go? I must direct the client to

where he or she feels a strong motivation to continue the journey: back to the "place" he or she came from before becoming incarnate in physical form. When the motivation is strong enough, the client will continue alone until she or he is received and welcomed home. The last piece, which the client travels alone, we call the Flower Bridge. It is not a bridge in the normal sense, and it is not made of, or decorated with, flowers, but appears as a brilliant arc of light in infinitely many colours. Not streaked like a rainbow, but, if seen with human eyes, it would appear as a bridge, covered in luminous flowers in thousands of colours.

We continue along the path that winds through a hilly landscape where Jacor continually adds new elements, trees, animals, sculptures, colours and light. It will be a work of art.

Suddenly I experience a flash, where everything turns black, as if someone turned off the lights at an art exhibition, but then we are back on the path. I feel a strong turmoil, and we agree to walk back to the garden where we are physically seated and making this dream walk landscape.

We are quickly back and take some deep breaths and drink water. Then I ask if my friends are okay.

"There was a moment of darkness," Janir says, which I confirm as also being my experience.

"I should be more at ease as we walked into the dream state," Jacor said. "The country's future concerned me and, when I saw the path, I came to ask: 'Where will the development we are currently experiencing lead the country?' Yes, just like a path leading somewhere. Suddenly I left my dream landscape and felt I was in another time, a possible future. I felt I was you," says Jacor and looks a little wondering at me.

"And I saw you, Yadar, and not Jacor in the dream," Janir says, "although I knew it was Jacor who experienced it."

"It may mean I don't even get the chance to experience this, but you, Yadar, have the chance, or, shall I say, are unfortunate to experience this terrible time. For yes, it was a terrible experience, even though I knew in a way it was kind of a dream."

"I only experienced the darkness for a short moment, but you experienced much more than that," I say.

"Yes," Janir says. "My experience, however, was that I was an observer of what Jacor, or you, experienced."

Azuru Timu

Here is the story Jacor tells us.

"I had worked twenty-four hours a day and had not been home with the family for a few days. Unfortunately, I had been so obsessed with my work I hadn't had time to relax and sit in silence. Had I listened to my body, it would have told me that something was wrong, but I did not have my thoughts with the family. Soon there were announcements that our families had been captured and rumours told about the most terrible things being done to them. It paralysed me when I focused on my loved ones. Everything went black in excruciating pain.

"In the past, our country was divided into areas, each with its own administration, and there was no central government for the country. The cultural and administrative centre was in what, far later, is called Mexico City. The man who became known as Azuru Timu had a dream of living forever and this was to be done in the way he knew, by taking life energy from other creatures. To do this effectively and without opposition from other areas, he first took over the whole country, Alt.

"Azuru Timu took the life energy from human beings by torture and sexual assault. People were kept for long-term suffering, because there was no intention to kill the energy source. The reason there was a particular focus on researchers was that we work with energy and maintain a healthy body and psyche. Azuru Timu knew that we had secrets which we kept for ourselves. There was no reason others outside the research community should have this knowledge as only we, the researchers, used it.

"We did not want to share our knowledge about the extension of life with Azuru Timu as it would mean that the country would have a brutal dictator for even more years. We could not, however, live with the suffering of our countrymen, and especially our loved ones.

"As representatives of the scientists, we were a small group who agreed to meet with the ruler's representatives. We were both insecure and frightened, but thought we had good cards in hand. The ruler had no reason to continue the atrocities when he gained the knowledge. We eventually made an agreement and wrote it down. All of us signed the document. Everything took place in a friendly and solemn atmosphere. Now we were just missing the ruler's consent and signature. It seemed like a formality, just one last hurdle before everything was well again.

"My superiors and I meet with the ruler in the palace itself and get the coveted signature. I do not understand why the ruler chose to wear a mask, and I also cannot reach into his thoughts. The atmosphere, however, feels fine, and there is beauty in the bright room, and there is food, drink and music. We will get the signature and soon after fetch our loved ones.

"As promised, they are all released, and we start healing processes to ease the effects of the torture. However, we will soon have something else to do, for they order us to meet in the temples of Tian to give our knowledge to the ruler's researchers.

"I am surprised to see the ruler himself present in the large auditorium, which we are banned from leaving until we pass all of our knowledge on. We are tired, but happy, when they finally allow us to go home, only to find that our families have once again been taken from us."

Here, Jacor ends the tale and we sit in the garden where Janir confirms it. We work to get back from the dream experience, after which I leave them. Jacor must, with the help of Janir, come to full clarity and find complete calm, both in terms of the future of our country and his own choice to end this life. I also contribute to this work, but from the temple the same afternoon.

In the evening, in my home, I ask to know what is going on, since it is just a possibility of a future. I slip away from the awakened state and meet a young man who, in some way, is myself. There is a huge number of glowing threads connected to the young man's back and they all disappear behind him in the darkness. Only one curls around to my left, and, as I follow the glowing thread with my eyes, I must finally turn my head and I see it ends up behind my back. It connects us, but why does he have so many threads, and I only this one? He smiles without commenting on the threads and continues the story that Jacor began earlier in the day, almost as if nothing had happened in the meantime.

"In my despair, I forget to take care of myself,

and before long we are all locked up. We all die in captivity, some of us after twenty or thirty years, after they have exposed us to the worst torments felt on this planet. Torments that still persecute us life after life. Eventually, however, the world gets peace from its oppressor. The ruler lived five hundred and fifty years before his madness became his death. Others have lived in his energy and accomplished terrible things throughout the ages, but, during his absence from Earth, the ruler's soul has worked to harmonise and draw wisdom out of the events. Now he prays for forgiveness and shares the wisdom he has reaped in his life as the ruler over Alt."

Then it becomes dark and empty around me and the communication is clearly over.

The story of Azuru Timu has made a great impression on me and I feel a knot of anxiety inside.

When I arrive at the temple the next day, I have decided not to share my knowledge of the powers of the magnetics with other people. This also means I cannot ask for help, but must work on this task alone.

I prepare for a meditation to give me a greater sense of what to do and what I can expect to happen in the future. I ask what happens after Jacor's story and get the following answer.

"The events around Azuru Timu will be the start of the country's final dissolution, both in terms of the last parts of the physical land and of the people who inhabit it. Smaller groups will venture out and start new communities around the globe and bring their knowledge to other peoples and help them in their development to a higher civilisation. Do not be concerned. Mankind will survive and find new ways … or perish and resurrect in its eternal quest for its highest potential."

Subsequently, I feel that Azuru Timu does not show up in this life, but lies as an option in the future of Alt. This means that it is more tied to the country than to me in another incarnations, as Jacor experienced during the initial dream walk.

Now it becomes clear that in my dreams and meditations I have been in both the past and a possible future. How is that possible? And how can I appear in the future if I die before things happen? I feel I am about to lose myself, that I am about to slip into a frenzy that will annihilate me.

"Who am I?" I ask.

"What are you?" is the answer.

"Stop!" I must stop my thoughts. They pull me down into a swirl of madness, a maelstrom I can never escape from. I get up fast, run out and take a cool bath. I stay in the bathtub until I can no longer stand the cold. The thoughts have stopped. There is only emptiness, and I feel a faintness throughout my body. I dry myself and go back to my room. I must lie down and just be, just sleep.

The boy with the mask

The young man with the lifelines is back, and a question comes up.

"How can you know something about the future unless it is predetermined, and where do the many threads connected to you go?"

"The future is not predetermined. Therefore, I don't tell you about your future. I tell you about my past. You have possibilities in front of you while I have experiences behind me. The many threads symbolise connections to many lives, which I, as a higher consciousness, have experienced. Now I gather the wisdom of those lives to integrate them into one entity, one consciousness."

The explanation about the future and the past makes perfect sense, but I can't connect the rest of what he says with anything.

"Please explain more about the threads. I can't get it into any context."

"I won't tell you about these connections as it's not relevant to what you're doing right now, but I'll tell you about something I experienced while I was a child in the life from which I now connect with you."

In what is now unfolding, it is I, Yadar, who experience the incident.

I am standing in a room. It's a living room. It is

warm and the rays of the sun find their way into the room through windows. There is a cosy and safe atmosphere. I sense I am a boy between eight and ten years old. There are no others in the house. The walls are of wood, or covered with wood, and the ceiling looks to be of wood as well. There is an archway into another room, but I remain in the living room. At first, I think I am standing on grass growing on the floor, but then I see it is a green carpet. The floor gives way a little under my feet. It is of wood as well. There is wooden furniture in the room and some chairs are upholstered. Close to the ceiling a shelf is put up on all four walls. Here I see books, various shapes and vases.

I hear the wind in the vegetation outside and look through the window. A narrow road divides the small garden from the inlet or fjord, with green waves topped with white foam.

A thought comes. "Why do I look through these eyes? Why did I choose to be in this body looking through its eyes? Why not another body and a different set of eyes? Would it make any difference?"

I understand I am not the body I inhabit, but the boy does not wonder what he is then, and why should he? He is the one he is! The one looking out through the eyes of the body he was born into.

I slip out of the dream, and, while I am between dream and the awakened state, I consider the experience to extract the wisdom or the message.

It's like wearing a mask that defines who I am, not only to others but also to myself. It is as if the mask works both ways, inward and outward.

It is one thing to realise how the mask works, and another to get the idea to change the mask, so a different person appears who you think fits what is deep inside you and is not affected by the world to the same degree. Again, both ways.

It appears that I am not me! Or I'm not the personality and the body I think I am … was. Who am I then? I come to think of the answer I received earlier when I asked who I am. The answer was a question: "What are you?" It was not WHO, but WHAT! … What?!

I'm not my body, okay. I am not a person. Hmm … it becomes difficult … or maybe I am several persons? No, if I were several persons, I would then know my I's! Or what? I must decide what a person comprises. I have a body, thoughts and emotions. I have my memories and my senses. As I cannot remember other lives immediately, I must not necessarily be my body with its senses, nor my emotions and thoughts. Yes, and the memory. Well, then there is nothing left!

Aha! I am the one who is behind the eyes as in the dream, he who travels in the dream, the dreamer. The one who IS. I am the conscious one, I am … consciousness!

Once again, I feel I am losing myself. Not to craziness this time, but to ecstasy!

This realisation overturns my worldview, my faith and the whole foundation of my existence. I am as if reborn, but to what? How does the world look, in fact? And, not least: Where do I come from?

My basic belief in life energy is still standing. I do not throw it out by my new insight. However, I must admit that it is not life energy that keeps me alive as consciousness. Life energy keeps alive all that lives on Earth, but as consciousness I am independent of life energy. I am not living on Earth. Meaning I can live without the Earth, without life energy!

Where does the life energy come from? We have been dealing with this issue for generations. The source obviously does not exist in the individual life forms. Even not in the air, as there are also living organisms in water.

It becomes necessary for me to meditate to get further clarity or to find answers in other ways. It becomes clear now I have learned that I am NOT my thoughts. But is consciousness not thoughts?

I slip into the darkness and the silence, feeling peaceful.

The man with the pointed hat

A person appears in front of me. He seems to stand in an arched doorway, and the wall is made of rocks. It is dark around us.

"Greetings!"

It is the friendly voice of a man. He wears a dark cowl and a weird pointed hat in the same dark colour as the cowl. The hat stands straight up and almost touches the lamp that emits a faint, yellow light in the surrounding darkness. His face hides in shadow.

"You are seeking answers that can help you out of the madness you feel lurking just beneath the surface of your mind."

"Oh, yes. I'm losing myself, losing my grip on what is me, and I'm feeling a deep fear of disappearing into nothingness, ceasing to exist."

"Nothingness contains everything."

"I don't understand."

"Understanding is thought in a mental context and, as you know, you are not your thoughts. Which, incidentally, is correct. Therefore, it should comfort you that it is only the part that is not you that does not understand."

"I understand that, but beyond that I still don't understand."

"The deeper understanding, the certainty, will

come to you, as small glowing pearls on a string. You will discover one pearl at a time, or all at once, as a sudden enlightenment. Probably both. The pearls first, and then you see the whole string of pearls and everything around it."

"And the pearls are the understanding of the experiences I have had lately?"

"Oh yes, but there have been other pearls you have not considered being yet another stone in the midstream that must lead you dry to the other bank … to the certainty and knowingness. The bank you are standing on now contains faith and doubt, two sides of the same coin. Faith is only a mental conviction that must be confirmed time and time again. The fact that faith must be continually affirmed shows that there is a profound doubt in faith."

I strongly feel I must have an answer to what I am.

"But if I'm neither my body, my thoughts nor my emotions, then I'm … nothingness? Am I nothing?"

"So true words. As I said, nothingness contains EVERYTHING, so you are EVERYTHING and not nothing. You have a conviction that if something should be something, it must be physical. You are right that you must be 'nothing', because in your innermost core you are not physical."

"How can this help me? I am more confused than before."

"Your anxiety lies in the fear of dying. Since dying is linked to your physical body, thoughts and emotions, it will require you to know you are not the body, the emotions and the mind. When this certainty occurs, the fear of death, and thus the fear of becoming nothing, disappears."

"How do I get this certainty? Can you help me?"

"No one can give you the certainty. It must come to you as a revelation, or an 'aha', if you will. Right now, you're very mental about this, so I would advise you to relax your thoughts and emotions, and to find the peace of your core. It is from here the knowingness will come."

The man takes a short break before he continues, "Here I will leave."

He bows, turns his back to me and leaves. When he is gone, the lamp turns off, and all light disappears. It happens so fast it feels almost like a vacuum has torn our dialogue apart. A rather strange way to end a meeting.

I am back in the darkness of my dreams, if possible more confused than before, but hoping what I have learned will bring more clarity when the time comes. There was no answer to the life energy. I must continue to work on this. The man with the pointed hat was really a personality, but much of what he said was in riddles, or as if he were speaking from a different, perhaps higher, understanding of the context of everything. I want to meet him again.

The answer to the divine

It is late morning. I sit in my study and think of the technology with magnets I and my people have forgotten. Is there anyone else who possesses this knowledge, or knowledge in general about our earliest history? Who do I know? It must be a deep secret since it has not come out. That makes it difficult to find anyone who even wants to admit that they know something.

Then I get an idea. "Janir, of course. I must ask her!" I flutter out of the room and reach halfway down the hallway before I realise that I am wearing my old sandals. I rush back for my nice sandals and sprinkle some floral water on my shoulders as well.

"I hope she's at home," I think to myself while struggling to get up the hill towards her and Jacor's home. A bell inside the house rings as I pull the string at the door.

"Gee, Yadar, I was just thinking about you."

Janir raises her head up over the hedge, smiles and brushes a lock of hair away from her face. She is in the middle of her gardening work.

"Janir, I must ask you something but not out here," I say breathlessly. I have, as always I suppose, forgotten about courtesy.

"Well, that's why I thought of you, right? Come inside, then we'll go into the backyard. And then I'd better get something refreshing for our sprinter." She smiles.

I don't know if she smiled because I didn't immediately understand who the sprinter was, or because of the stupid expression on my face until I realised that it was me she alluded to. I must say in my defence that, since being an adult, nobody has ever called me a sprinter.

When we sit at the table and the girl who brought the refreshments has left, I remember I have not seen Jacor.

"Isn't Jacor here?"

"No, he went on one of his trips after breakfast. I probably won't see him until late in the afternoon. Don't worry. He's fine. Now, let me hear what made you sprint up the mountain to visit me."

"Yes," I say in a low voice and bend towards her. "You know many people, so I wonder if you might know someone who knows something about our earliest history. Maybe something most others no longer remember."

"I can tell from your whisper that it is not ordinary history that interests you. It is about the rejuvenation through magnetic influence, right?"

Janir looks very serious.

"Well, I thought I could use a confirmation that what I have experienced is not just a crazy dream. It will give me a better sense of where I stand."

Janir cocks her head. "Oh yes, but it won't make your situation easier. If you get confirmation that the rejuvenation practice has taken place, you are in a very dangerous situation if you do anything in that direction. Am I right?"

While I speak, I feel over-zealous and nervous at the same time. "Obviously, Janir, but I must know. I can't live with that doubt."

"Certainly. I have one person in mind, but I must contact him first. This is dangerous. Not only for us, but for anyone who may be suspected of withholding information. Therefore, let us agree that I will inquire about the possibility of a meeting, and then you let me know the outcome afterwards. I will meet you in the temple when I know an answer."

"Thanks, Janir. It's hard to emphasise what it really means to me. I hope you understand."

"I do, but don't thank me yet. It may turn out that you have made an unfortunate choice."

Then we engage in small talk, but I cannot concentrate and I say goodbye after a short while. I know that Janir understands.

Back in my study in the temple I wander restlessly back and forth between the bookcase at one end and the sideboard at the other. I already have several bruises on the thighs from, in my distraction, walking into the table's edge as it stands a little too close to the route I choose to trudge.

"Pull yourself together. It may take days before you get to know anything. It is uncertain that this person is easy to meet, and he or she may not be living here in Tian."

I stop at the table, pour a glass of water and drip a

little lime juice in it. "Ah," I say, when I have emptied the glass. I close my eyes, sigh and try to relax.

"Deep breaths always help to rest the body, thoughts and emotions."

It is Janir's voice. Why has Cantor not announced her arrival? Or have I not heard him?

I open my eyes and turn towards the doorway.

"Welcome, Janir, but where is Cantor?"

"Oh, I did not report my arrival to him. It is best so." She looks serious. "I have spoken to someone who has agreed to meet with you."

Janir whispers the address and disappears quickly out the door again.

Everything has been going so fast. I sit down to make a plan, but I immediately get up again. I need to leave. I have to continue my search.

After making myself presentable, I tell Cantor I don't know when I will be back. He is used to that so that is no problem. He also knows I happen to forget the time, which really gets to me. I make some stops on the way, greeting acquaintances and even chatting with a café owner whom I know well, while I drink a cup of tea at a table outside the café.

At last I approach the destination. I stop myself from looking around. It will only seem suspicious. Instead I spend some time checking my garments while taking a discreet look around. There are people around me, but no one seems to take any notice of me. I step through a narrow gate and enter a small yard that turns out to be empty. Opposite the gate is the wooden door to the house. A narrow window is placed on each side of the door. A blue arch is painted on the brickwork around the door, like a door frame, and the arch is decorated with irregular yellow stars. The arch is irregular at the edges as well.

Janir didn't give the name of the person, so I must believe that the person who opens the door is the one with whom I must speak. There is no bell, so I knock on the door and wait.

I hear dragging steps behind the door. An elderly man opens and shade his eyes against the bright sunlight with his hand and we make eye contact.

"I'm Yadar."

"Well, please come in. I was just about to make tea when you knocked."

I follow him inside and close the door behind us. The man is tall and slightly bent. He wears a blue cowl, with the hood hanging down his back. We enter a small living room where the man points to a chair at the table.

"Sit down, Yadar, and take a glass of water. You must be thirsty in the heat. Then I'll pour water over the tea for it to infuse."

After I have poured water in my glass, I look around the small living room. A cosy place, spartan furnishings. He seems to live here alone. He must be the one I am here to talk to. Suddenly everything stops. The pointed hat from the dream sits on the sideboard in one corner of the living room. It is in the shadows, so I hadn't noticed it right away.

"Welcome. My name is Memton, by the way. Hey, what's wrong?"

"Did we meet the other night in a dream?"

"Well, not that I know of, but your unconscious or, more precisely, your higher consciousness, can be several places at the same time, both when you sleep and when awake. So maybe we met. That is, a part of your consciousness remembers the meeting and a part of my consciousness doesn't remember it."

"First, I must know if a certain person has agreed that I can meet with you and talk about a problem I have."

"Yes, I've been told that you would show up in a short time. You are a real sprinter, I was told."

I nod. This is the person that Janir thought could help me. Now I am curious if he is the man whom I met in my dream. In few words I tell him about the meeting and that the person had a similar cowl, and not least the pointed hat.

He faces me after putting the teapot on the table.

"First, we must make out some basic things before we can go ahead with what you actually came here for; or it might be really the basic things that will turn out to be what takes you further on your quest."

I look impatiently at him as he continues.

"It may well be a part of me that has brought about this conversation with you. The things being passed on I well know of. However, I lean more towards the explanation that it is a part of you that you had this dialogue with. This part might also have given you clues, like a man, a blue cowl and a pointed hat. These were the things you could use to find me. It was not quite the way it played out, but perhaps the energy of the dream was to give your acquaintance the idea it was me you should contact. It may be difficult for you to understand this right now, but it will become clearer later. I sense we have a lot to talk about, some parts of which are absolute secrets. Do you understand that?"

I nod. "Yes, I understand the severity and necessity of anything remaining secret, but how do you know you can trust me?"

Memton has poured tea into two mugs and given me one. I try the tea, but it's still too hot. It smells nice, spicy without my being able to work out the ingredients.

"I trust the one who asked for you and I follow my intuition that tells me I can talk about topics beyond the ordinary, and that I must convey some of my knowledge to you."

The seriousness is clear in his voice, but I also sense a keenness, and perhaps also a relief he has someone with whom he can share his knowledge.

Memton continues, "Before we can get on with something else, we need to talk about consciousness and what that concept covers." He lifts the mug with tea, puffs over it and takes a careful sip.

"What do you think about the tea?"

I lift the mug, puff and sip a little. "It is lovely; and spicy. What's in it?"

"That's my secret recipe. You can get a bag, so it's not that big a secret, but let me talk about consciousness." He clears his throat. "When you are awake, you are aware of yourself and the things that happen around you. Let's call it your daytime consciousness. When you're asleep, you're unconscious about the things happening around you and in your body, but you can be aware of what's happening in a dream. You may also be aware that what you are experiencing is a dream, right?"

"Certainly, but I think there is a difference between what we could call an ordinary dream, and, for example, the meeting I had with the man with the pointed hat, or many other experiences I have had and of which I will tell you later. You may know a little from Janir?" I look inquiringly at him.

"We only talked briefly, but she mentioned that you have these experiences. It's as it should be. You can relax."

After a larger sip of the tea this time, he continues, "Let's start by establishing that you are conscious. Not your thoughts and feelings, or anything else that may be associated with the body and its personality. All this disappears when you die. I assume you are this far in your reasoning."

"I am, but I may not have had it quite so succinctly formulated for myself."

There is a short break while I try to formulate a question.

"Why am I not my thoughts? How else can I think when I'm not in the physical?"

"Thoughts are in the physical, and although it may feel like they are fast, you know it takes time to think. Consciousness's 'thoughts' and the true creating act are instantaneous. It doesn't take time for consciousness to think or to create."

Memton can see I have more to say, so he takes another sip of his tea and nods towards me. "Continue. The more you can formulate yourself, the easier it is for you to move forward in your understanding."

"When I make a dream walk, it is not with the person or personality, but with the person's consciousness. Yes, and my consciousness, or is that wrong?"

"It's close. You have to remember that the personality still, so to speak, clings on to the assumption it is the person who needs to move on after death. Only when there is so much awareness present that the higher consciousness can escape from the personality and the body is it the pure consciousness that makes the journey. The personality cannot move on, but must be dissolved and distilled or, should I say, transformed into wisdom, which is the consciousness's award for a lifetime spent as a person. If a personality is unconscious about his own mortality and the immortality of consciousness, it can linger in the vibratory field above the physical world, being aware or unaware that it is no longer in the physical world. Therefore, the dream walk

50

and, above all, the preparation is so important."

"You mentioned the higher consciousness. Explain this in more detail."

"Let's prepare a meal while we talk further."

Memton walks to the table where he prepares food. I follow him. He finds a loaf of bread in a cloth bag and gives it to me together with a knife. I cut two slices each while he continues his elucidation.

"Imagine that your daytime consciousness is only a small part of your collective consciousness, and that this daytime consciousness is isolated from the higher consciousness. This happens to give the personality the impression that everything it can sense is all that is."

"Yes, but in reality there is more beside consciousness is moving on after death? … Oh, I've experienced that I have different lives. Is that the secret?"

I get very anxious and cut the last slice of bread rather skewed.

"It is part of the secret, but it is the secret behind the secret that is interesting. So, why's it a secret? The interesting thing is that it need not be a secret. People may reach the conclusion by themselves: that there is much more to life than one can sense through one's three-dimensional sensory system with its three-dimensional brain and reasoning."

Memton is preparing vegetables and asks me to rinse some fruit from a bowl on a shell on the wall above our heads.

"Should I cut it up?"

"No, no. Just rinse it and wipe it. There is a clean cloth hanging there."

It is perhaps because of the skewed piece of bread that he prefers that I do not use the knife. "Stop it. Don't think like that, you blockhead," I think to myself.

Memton has finished the vegetables and puts them on the dining table along with various savoury oils, spices and salt. There is a jug of fresh water on the table as well. I add the fruit and the bread slices and make sure that the skewed slice is closest to me. When we sit at the table, each with a portion of food, Memton says, "I will continue while we eat, as there is much we must cover."

I nod while I munch.

"Can you imagine that there is one highest consciousness which, so to speak, is common to all consciousness?"

"God." It comes out of me. Unfortunately, along with some food. "I have experienced this concept on my journeys in consciousness. And now that the life force is not in the body … or is it? Does the life force come from the highest consciousness?"

"We must tread carefully here, and therefore I will postpone my answer about the life force for later, perhaps another day, and continue talking about consciousness. But, yes, we can call this highest consciousness god's consciousness, the creative consciousness."

"Yet another proof that my experience is not just my imagination," I think, as I wipe the food from the table that flew out of my mouth at my sudden outburst.

"I have a thought, now we have mentioned the concept of god. I have come across the idea that one must save one's soul. Is this the consciousness you have talked about?"

"Hmm." Memton frowns. "Our higher consciousness need not be saved from anything, so I don't know what that means. You might find out on your inner journeys yourself."

"How do you know so much about consciousness? Do you also have visions and inner journeys like me?"

"I am not so much a gatherer of information, but more one who holds the 'forgotten' wisdom that can be passed on when our world is to benefit from it without abusing it. I feel that something very dark is coming, and that it is more important than ever before to keep this wisdom secret."

It seems as if a shadow passes in front of his face and it fills his eyes with grief. Then he straightens up, stands, takes the teapot and walks to the kitchen table. "How about a mug of hot cocoa?" he says with a cheerful voice, as if to sweep away the gloomy darkness.

"That would be great," I say, and know there is still a lot to go through. I stand, stretch and walk over to the pointed hat. "Where does the hat come from? I have seen nothing like it before."

"Funny you ask. It is from a dream I do not remember, but when I had to make a triangular hat, I remembered it from the dream. A triangular hat becomes a cone in the three-dimensional world."

While Memton stirs the cocoa, he continues, "Consciousness does not need time and space to exist, so we can say the divine consciousness has always existed. In the following parable I will use words that refer to time, space and place, because they are necessary to provide an explanation that the brain can understand."

Memton pours the cocoa in two clean mugs. We return to the dining table and he continues, "The divine consciousness knows itself as a self-awareness, but not as a human will know itself through the body's senses, its thoughts and emotions. The first desire to experience itself arises, and the divine consciousness can gather its various properties into two parts of itself, the feminine and the masculine we may call it, letting each part experience the other. At this first meeting, a great love is experienced for the other part, and the desire to experience this ecstasy again and again occurs. If we always know what we will experience, it is not a new experience, therefore the two parts now create offspring of consciousness with the same characteristics and a veil, so they do not remember their divine parents. The offspring of consciousness are sent into a void to experience the first meeting where they recognise themselves in the other. At the same time as the desire to experience love and oneself in all shapes or aspects arises, the divine gets a taste for creating. All of its offspring therefore receive the divine creator's abilities, so they are true images of the divine.

There is no difference except that they do not re-member their ancestry. At some point, there came a need to create an environment where creation, action and reaction take place very slowly, with re-spect to the instantaneous which the consciousness up to that point has experienced. It then creates a three-dimensional universe with time, space and other rules we know. To be faithful to the true ex-perience of this slow environment, each conscious-ness lays a veil over what it really is, in relation to the creatures they must act through. This is the sto-ry, almost as short as it can be and therefore very deficient."

Emotions overwhelm me.

"Well, with this parable I see a larger continuity, but it will take some time before it settles in."

"Certainly, but I have grown tired of this much talking. Let's say you come back tomorrow, but not too early. I need time to get up and do my stuff."

I grab Memton's hand.

"Thank you very much for your time, wisdom and energy. We both need to rest after this visit. See you tomorrow."

The old man sees me to the door. We say no more; only a nod, and then I disappear into the shadows of the evening.

It's a cold night and I freeze. Or is it a reaction to the many impressions I've received? I hurry home; no one sees me arrive. I go straight to the couch, kick off my sandals and lie on on my back with my clothes on. Sigh.

There was no answer to the magnetic therapy. As Memton said, it was of greater importance for my total overview to first know more about consciousness.

Sleep comes faster than expected. Later in the night I wake, urinate, drink some water and take off my clothes. The heat has returned to my body.

The start of my existence

The next morning, I am very clear in the head, but exhausted in the body. Hmm, shouldn't it be the other way around? I'm passionate about telling Janir about the meeting, but know well I can't talk to anyone about these things. However, I do not fully understand why I must not share it. That will be one of my questions for the next meeting with Memton.

After taking a bath, making things ready for the day and eating a light breakfast, I feel no encouragement to go to the temple. The sun sends its heat and its light into the room and I decide to go back to the moment when I went from being the god's consciousness or everything to becoming a conscious self. I make myself comfortable and remember that it was love that the consciousness of god experienced. With the clear intention to experience my first birth and meet the god consciousness in a loving embrace, I settle my thoughts and focus on my breath.

I had thought it would be difficult to bring my consciousness "back" to this moment, but just by focusing on it, or, rather, turning my own love toward divine love, only a few seconds pass before I am in a sense of unconditional love, where I experience myself drifting from the Divine Mother to the "arms" of the Divine Father, who greets me. "You are." My consciousness is completely clean and empty. Then comes the wonderful thought: "I exist!" I shall now experience life through the aspect of god, myself. I do, however, have the feeling

I have existed before this moment, just not as me. Therefore, I am not created by the Divine Mother and Father, but I am a part of them, a part of which has now gained its own consciousness. The I, who has now its own consciousness, is not separate from what I was. We are still connected and therefore I have always existed.

I don't want to leave this feeling, but I slowly slip away and send, with gratitude, my love toward the love I come from.

Slowly I open my eyes. I feel an internal warmth that matches the warmth of the sun that touches me through the open window. I am happy. I am at home, and not because I am in my physical home. It is huge. Is that all it takes? Is it all I must do to meet my true parents? Of course, it is not a woman and a man, feminine and masculine, but the divine consciousness that is in all of us.

After a while I pour a glass of water, get up slowly and walk to the window while I drink. I feel empty, but in a good way. I have found peace for a while. Then Memton appears in my thoughts. I leave the window, take another glass of water, drink it and prepare to go on my second visit to the man with the pointed hat.

The small god

The common consciousness

I step into the new day's dazzling sunshine and walk at a calm pace towards the temple. I must see Cantor and check up on queries, and whatever else might wait for me, and inform him of my plans for the day. I have chosen not to keep my meetings with Memton a secret from Cantor. It will make things more difficult and, as no one knows he has this knowledge, my actions will raise suspicions. We must find an acceptable subject to talk about.

It is late morning when I knock on the door encircled by the blue arch with the stars. Memton answers the door. "Well, hello, dear Yadar. Come on in."

He holds the door for me this time and I walk straight into the small living room. The pointed hat is in the same position as the last time I saw it.

"We must choose a common interest we can discuss," I say and turn towards him.

"Tea and water?" he asks. "Sit down. Oh, I forgot to give you the bag of tea before you left last night. Here it is."

"Yes, thanks, and thanks for the tea. I shall put the tea should in my shoulder bag right away." I open my shoulder bag which is now hanging on the backrest of the chair where I sit.

Memton places nuts and dried fruit on the dining table and then fetches a jug of water. I take glasses and mugs from the shelf above the kitchen table and return to the table.

While Memton prepares the tea, and therefore stands with his back to me at the kitchen table, he says, "A harmless but also plausible subject that is of interest to us both? What do you work with? Crystals, energy, dream walking?"

"Yes, these are topics we can use. I have questions about life energy, with an angle in relation to the new knowledge given to me."

I pick up the jug and pour water for both of us. Soon, Memton joins me at the table, on which he puts the tea pot.

"I will continue where I left off yesterday and introduce a new concept, that of mass consciousness or common consciousness. That is a consciousness that all we share. I would like to point out that, although each of our consciousnesses has no scope or form, it can be said that it is in the space between the building blocks of our three-dimensional world. Our consciousness is, so to speak, woven into this world, but is not of this world. When a person thinks or feels something, it becomes part of a common consciousness. Therefore, you must understand that the common consciousness contains everything all human beings have thought and felt and all of our unwritten rules, morals, dogmas and prejudices or beliefs. Here are all habits and vices, lusts and desires. Not only do all of us contribute to this 'soup', we are also constantly affected by it.

It is therefore extremely important that we must be clear about our own feelings and thoughts, and what we can let go because it does not belong to us. What you pick up from common consciousness feels as strong and personal as if it were your own. You must therefore determine if what you feel and think is your own. You can only be influenced by something in the common consciousness that you already know or are open to, otherwise you will not attract it."

"You need to explain a bit more. Why can I only be affected by something that I already know or am open to? It sounds pretty strange."

"I will answer you briefly and then clarify it later. You see, what you have experienced works as a magnet on the things that are in the common consciousness. It is the same thing that happens when someone is not aware of how things work and then is reborn. You are born into the same energies that your energy field contains. This applies the other way too when one dies. Namely, you are drawn towards the same energies that your energy field contains when you die. If you think there is nothing after death, then your consciousness ends up in 'nothing'. Here you will stay until you find that you still exist even though you are dead. I will not go into these matters in detail now, but will continue the direction I was on, and later we can return to the behaviour of attraction."

"Yes, of course. Please continue, but we must certainly return to this subject of attraction later."

"Common awareness is not uniform, but varies

from area to area. Each town is different, each part of a town is different, each country is different and so on. It is culture specific. The awareness connects to the area where it is created although it itself has no scope or physical characteristics."

"I imagine it as little clouds. At the 'bottom' they connect with a bigger cloud that then reassembles into one big cloud. At the 'top' there is the common consciousness for the entire planet," I say.

"It's an excellent picture. The difference between the common consciousness and your higher consciousness is that you, who are the real you, are the god-consciousness that also has its creator abilities. However, common awareness is produced by the personalities of mankind, their thoughts, feelings, fears and desires. One could say that it is a primitive being."

"Perhaps it can be described as a huge personality," I add.

"Yes, certainly. It is a human personality without a soul. As the common consciousness has grown ever larger, it sees itself as an independent creature with power over humanity. To some extent, this awareness is right, as mankind is influenced by it. It feels like a god; as the god over mankind. It is, however, an artificial consciousness without creative force. It is created by mankind and belongs to humanity, and not the other way around. If mankind was aware of this and each took responsibility for their own life, the common consciousness would have no influence, no power."

"That sounds pretty creepy, I think."

I get shivers when thinking of this creature that has such power over mankind, even if it is mankind who has created the beast itself; even if it is done unconsciously. I would really like to hear more, but the juice from the fruit, the water and the tea has eventually filled my bladder, so I must ask Memton to take a break so I can bring this in order.

"Yes, of course. I myself also have this need. You first. Go through the door there. When you reach the end of the hallway you are there. I'll let in some fresh air."

He points to a door that is opposite the entrance, which leads to the rear part of the house. Shortly after, I am back in the living room and then it is Memton's turn. He, however, returns and continues where he left off with his story about the common consciousness.

"As you are affected by the common consciousness, you can also influence it. It is here that it becomes really interesting. This means that you can influence humanity with your insights and wisdom to raise self-awareness, so that each human has the conscious choice to control his or her own life, rather than letting the common consciousness dictate it. The individual, however, must reach some maturity to be able to benefit from the wisdom. This is linked to what I said about the fact that we are attracting what we contain. For example, let's say you need to contain half the wisdom before you can start to take advantage of it and thereby accelerate your growth."

"Well, as a human being, don't I decide over my

own life? I definitely don't feel like I'm being controlled by anything outside me."

"Sorry, but you don't decide as much as you think. What you do in your life is more a reaction to what you are experiencing. If you decide, you act; you don't respond. Let us take an example where you have an unpleasant experience. You feel uncomfortable. The question is whether the feeling arises because you recognise the experience as something you have experienced before, with the unpleasant feeling as a result, or is it the common consciousness that connects to your sense of feeling and 'transfers' its own feeling of the situation. Is the episode really uncomfortable in objective terms, or is it just feelings that get in your way, so you don't see the situation objectively? So, what controls your reaction? Where does it come from?"

"You really give me something to think about."

"Humans are governed by their emotions, and emotions arise from thoughts and inner images. Here I must make a side note about memory. Experiences are stored both in the brain's memory and in the body's memory. The processing of experiences stored in the body's memory often occurs as a reflex. You do not use the brain to think of such a reaction. It is the body that reacts outside your intellect. As you have experienced, body reflexes are much quicker than thought to lead to a reaction. We can say that the body has its own consciousness, but I think that Janir can tell you more about the body."

"I will certainly ask her about the body's memory

when I next get the opportunity."

"It takes great insight into the nature of life to get beyond this game, this control from the outside. A person must be conscious and awake and be quicker than his mental and bodily reflexes. This can only be done by acting as consciousness, since consciousness, as previously mentioned, is immediate and therefore is quicker than both thoughts and bodily reflexes."

"Living seems to be much more chaotic and extensive than I had imagined."

"Oh, there you are wrong. People see it as chaotic and make it very difficult for themselves. Although life as a human being has been built up in a complex system with many layers and connections, it can be lived very simply and with much fullness if you live consciously."

Here I get a chance to tell Memton about my experience of my own beginning as consciousness that I had had last night. He listens with great interest and nods occasionally, and I sense that he forms some inner images of the tale.

"It must have been a great experience for you. This gives me the opportunity to tell you that you will not return to the unity with this father and mother consciousness. You will remain a unique and independent consciousness. The yearning you may feel isn't your yearning to become one with these parents, but your higher consciousness' yearning to be united with you, the human aspect!"

"The search for a god that I have experienced on

my 'journeys', in fact, is every human's search for himself, a quest to be united with himself. It also means there is actually no higher god to find."

"Only when every human finds itself will it realise that the god they have sought does not exist. They are their own god, you can say. I can imagine that for a moment there will be a disappointment, which is then followed by a sense of total freedom and sovereignty, when this realisation has settled."

Difference between feelings and emotions

"I will briefly talk about emotions. As mentioned earlier, emotions are part of the personality and not of consciousness. This is not quite correct. Imagine that we distinguish between feelings and emotions, where emotions are what the personality experiences as feelings, which are reactions to thoughts and chemistry produced in the brain, while feelings are you as consciousness sensing. Just as your body has physical senses, consciousness has senses as well, just many more; over 200,000. It is these senses I call feelings. One of them we call genuine compassion, which is your unconditional acceptance of another human being and its choices."

"So, emotions come from thoughts?"

"Emotions and thoughts are in a sense the same. Thoughts lead to emotions and they act as amplifiers of thoughts. In this way, these two things run in a loop. Both come as reactions to events that the mind experiences in the outer or inner world."

It is now past noon and I must return to the temple and attend an event. I thank Memton for his time and wise words and leave the cosy living room, this time with the tea in my shoulder bag. I am reluctant to walk out into the heat, but I can walk in the shadows most of the time. On my way back, I can't help thinking about what Memton has told me.

It is terrifying that the common consciousness that humanity has created, to a great degree, deludes us into how our world is, rather than that each human chooses her or his life. I see a painting for me, painted by the common consciousness. This painting is being hung in front of all people and they then live in the belief that the world looks like this. Not only now, but in the future as well. We do not remove the painting, and we rarely revise it.

Emotions and thoughts are therefore two sides of the same coin, and they can intensify each other. In this way, an experience that started as a reaction in the mind can eventually grow out of proportion.

The land of white

It's been a long day, but now I finally lie on my cotton-stuffed mattress. It's been a hot day as well, and I try to imagine a cool breeze against my face while breathing the cold air through my nose. It doesn't quite work, but this focus makes my mind relax and I glide into the depths of my dreams.

I find myself in an Arctic area, all white from the reflections of light in snow and ice. The sun is shining, the sky is blue, and the colour thins out until it turns white on the horizon and joins with the white landscape. I turn from my position as an observer to become a person in this white place.

I am filled with great joy and pride and look at my little son, all dressed in white bear skins. I smile. He is almost as wide as he is tall. His legs look even shorter than usual when he is wrapped in all that fur. I feel a great love for life. That's what kids do. They make us feel love. It is their first and greatest mission in life.

The sled is laden and the dogs are impatient to get on the way. I check the traces one last time and make eye contact with the lead dog, a large female. We have confidence in each other and now it is up to us if we arrive.

We will, along with others, on sledges, pulled by dogs, to a gathering with other clans from a large area.

She comes stooping out of the hut and stands upright. She smiles and I see the words in her eyes:

"You are proud and happy and I am also." How I love this woman!

It is the first time he will be on the sled, my first-born, but he knows what will happen. He has heard many stories in the short time he has been with us, and I know that he himself will tell stories of his life long after I have left this life.

I remember the dream when I wake up. It was a wonderful scene, both emotionally and as an experience of being in the special, white nature. I felt a great peace, devotion and love. It had to be a simple life, though, with much focus on survival.

During breakfast I decide I will once again visit Memton. First I must visit the temple and check up on some things. There is nothing of great importance and I can be with Memton before it gets too hot.

Uniformity and unification

Once again I sit in Memton's cosy living room, each of us with a cup of tea. I wait for him to begin his story.

After taking a cautious sip of the hot tea, Memton takes an almost theatrical breath and speaks with a serious voice.

"What I am telling you is now forbidden knowledge and therefore deadly dangerous. At the beginning of the Alt period there was a great variety of human types, both in appearance and size. Some were very tall and others quite small. They had evolved through the Mu period, i.e., the period before we emigrated from Mu. Slowly, the idea of creating a more uniform human type arose and we began to create the perfect body. When I look at the human body today, I must say that we did a fantastic piece of work. We adjusted everything to the slightest detail, to achieve the greatest goal of success in relation to the opportunities that exist on the planet. We are indeed creators.

"Later it went awry. That happened when we adjusted the brain's capacity to create the most intelligent citizens so they had the best ability to contribute to the benefit of the country. We drove this to the extreme when the nation's elite made brain alterations to be superior in intelligence compared to the rest of the population. To create an even larger boundary, they made metal and magnet headbands to control parts of the population. They introduced this 'coronation' as a privilege, with different symbols for different groups. They did this to cover up the actual purpose. They also made alterations to the brain, with various kinds of blockages for further control.

"For generations, these blockages, both those that were effected by the headbands and those with surgery, were hereditary. These adjustments found their way to the common consciousness and all subsequent generations are affected by this. Even a person who has not been subjected to a headband or physical surgery receives these blockages, even today."

With this, Memton ends his story and we sit in silence for a long time. He gives me plenty of time to get over the shock of this information. I am shocked. Then we take a short walk into the yard to clear the mind and emotions before we, once again, sit down at the table in the living room.

I start the conversation.

"When humanity is ready, as in mature, for the wisdom, it will find it, because it is in the common consciousness. Neither you nor anyone else need to pass the wisdom from generation to generation. Let go of this burden. It will destroy you."

Memton nods thoughtfully.

"The problem is that these blockages prevent the wisdom from being brought into the mind of humanity. There must be someone who knows the blockages to bring this knowledge to the people of the world through the common consciousness."

Now I understand his concern. I nod and tell about the magnet rejuvenation I experienced in the icy room, far up in the mountain.

Memton is silent while I am speaking, waiting to comment when I am done.

"It's very interesting that you get an insight into these things and that you get fair answers to your questions. Who do you think is communicating with you?"

"First, I felt that there were many people who contributed, but now I think my higher consciousness is the primary voice."

Memton rubs his chin.

"The many can be the wisdom from many lives you then perceive as individuals."

"That sounds like a very plausible explanation."

"Oops, we forgot lunch. I have some soup from yesterday, and I will walk to the baker for a loaf of bread. The soup is in the jar over there, and you can take a pot from under the kitchen table. Maybe you can clear the table too?"

"Yes, sure. I know where the things are now."

While Memton fetches the bread, I warm the soup and clear the table.

It's not long before Memton is back, filling the room with a fragrance of freshly baked bread.

"Here's the bread. When I walked back from the bakery, I had the idea that a glass of wine would fit fine with the soup. What do you say?"

"Oh, that sounds nice. I'll put two glasses on the table."

Memton fetches a jar of white wine from the basement and soon we sit and enjoy the meal.

Energy

Memton does not waste time, so when we are ready to eat, he explains about energy.

"Energy is not life, so we cannot talk about life-force energy. Energy is the building block the consciousness uses in its creations. Everything is built with attributes that tells how the thing should be perceived. A thing is not a THING, but INFORMATION to the receiving awareness of how to perceive it. Take the pot here, for example. It appears with a shape, hardness and surface, and other properties, such as the tendency to break if dropped. It is the same energy that has created the water, but with quite different properties. Consciousness creates the jug and water, and both have self-awareness and are conscious of what they are in immediate contact with."

"But isn't it the potter who made the pot?"

"Yes, and the potter is also consciousness, and the clay is part of the planet that has also been created."

Life force energy

"What about the charging of energy in the body using the crystal bed in the pyramid?" I ask.

"It is the limited human consciousness that wants the energy of the body and this is not very effective because of its limitations. The restriction arises because of the lack of understanding of energy and how consciousness works."

"What is your comment about my dream of rejuvenating body cells using magnets in relation to energy?"

"The rejuvenation takes place or was conducted with a deeper understanding of how to create. The magnets assisted in transferring the properties of the young cells to the degraded cells, which then used this information at cell division."

Memton pours more wine into the glasses before he continues.

"What happens at the crystal bed in the pyramid is only a recharge and not a change of the cells. A transfusion of a young person's blood will, in my opinion, have a greater effect than the pyramid."

Memton offers a final remark before I leave him. "We cannot have a decadent elite who can maintain their power by having a long and healthy life. It is therefore of the utmost importance that what we are talking about should not be brought forward. This also means we cannot use this knowledge ourselves."

A nature's being as a human

Here is an experience I want to share with you.

At one point I come across an elderly woman who is very rigid in her perception of right and wrong. Not only with morals but also how things are done on a daily basis. For her, there is only one right way to do things and she can react strongly if this is not done. It seems it causes her pain to see something done "wrong".

At some point I realise that I might have known her from another life. As I am curious about this, I ask one evening in a meditation for the cause of her reactions.

"She is originally a being of nature," is the answer.

Because I do not understand this concept, I must ask for elaboration. I get a longer answer, which I relate below.

The being of nature inhabits the planet just like humans, but while humans generally withdraw themselves from close bonds with the planet, the being of nature lives in close contact with nature where their work is. They are NOT the animals occupying the planet. They are usually not perceived by humans and are therefore invisible to you. This has not always been the case, but since people are very dominant and destructive, they caused the beings of nature a great deal of pain, so the beings asked to be moved from the world of mankind. The higher authorities fulfilled this request by shifting them slightly away from the field of human consciousness; in fact, what you are working with.

Nature works according to very specific rules, and as the creatures of nature live so close with nature, their rules of life are very similar to nature. Although nature is diverse and experimental, there are still basic rules that must be followed.

The woman's soul had always been reborn as a creature of nature; both as a woman and a man. In recent lives, in the days after the beings of nature were separated from mankind, she had been very frustrated with the awful behaviour and way of life of humans, and she had several times complained about this, both when she was in a life and to her master after a life.

"Why can't people learn to treat each other and nature with love?" she asks her master shortly after she returned from a life on Earth. "Something must be done!" she says in despair.

The master answers that mankind will eventually mature and find love for everything, including nature, but she must be patient. Usually, beings of nature are patient, but this being turned back again and again to her master with the same frustration, so the master suggested that she could be reborn as a human being, for only through another human being could the "blind" be turned towards love.

"Never in any life will I be human!" she replied with disdain every time her master presented the proposal. At one point, however, the idea had taken so much root in her that she eventually agreed to try. She knew exactly what she would do. "And they must listen to reason!"

However, it is one thing to be a higher consciousness with its full potential, and another thing to be incarnated with only a tiny part of this consciousness in the world's heaviness as a human being. So, when she incarnated, she forgot most of what she had set out to do, but pursued through several incarnations a heartfelt desire to teach mankind "the proper way of living". She felt that what she experienced as a human being was wrong, but she did not understand why she responded so strongly, and felt she did not know herself when, soon after, she looked back at an event that had brought her out of her composure.

Now it made sense, and I was ready with my next question.

"I feel a great respect or affection towards this human being, as if I have known her earlier. Can I get any information about this?"

"You've had more lives in what you call the land of white, and in one of these lives you and she were a husband and wife, where you were the woman in this relationship. Your husband sacrificed everything for the family, obtained food and protected it, but he was also very demanding. You see, he did everything he could for the family's survival and saw his hardness as a necessity for this survival. You therefore had a great devotion and what you would call love for your husband, even though you were afraid of him as well."

The dream walk

I have had meetings with Janir and Jacor where we focused on Jacor's transition and dream walk and all the details are now in place.

It can be hard for outsiders to understand why Jacor has chosen to leave Janir, the woman whom he has known just about his entire life. This requires a deeper knowledge of the couple and the ties between them. Death cannot break these strong bonds. I must confess that I have had to work to accept Jacor's decision to move towards, as he says, "something greater that I reconcile with and where I, through this greater, can contribute in countless ways to improve life on the planet. Janir and I have always been, and will always be, connected. Even the idea that we shall meet AGAIN seems absurd because we are not separated."

The couple have always fully accepted each other, which also means that Janir, as the wise woman she is, has accepted her life companion's decision to leave the physical world.

The prelude to a dream walk starts the night before, with a celebration for and with Jacor. Few and very close friends are invited and, with a focus on joy and renewal, we are together this evening.

The few guests and I stay overnight and the next morning the preparations for the actual dream walk continue.

During the night, Jacor has been surrounded by light, tones and fragrances to make him relax and bring him to a mood of satisfaction and with the feeling that everything is as it should be. The food he ate during the feast was prepared for the same effect. After breakfast, they treat his skin with oils of various kinds. This also causes the body to feel safe and willing to separate from the consciousness that has inhabited it throughout its existence. The body must feel revered, in the same way as the consciousness that is shortly to leave it. I, who thought I knew everything about dream walking, have learned a lot in a short time. I have a different view of the process. As I see it, the body is a sovereign creature, albeit partly guided by consciousness.

Janir and I have maintained contact with Jacor throughout the night, assisted by the other people. Now Janir, Jacor and I focus on the dream walk landscape that I, from Jacor's wishes, have created and maintained for the purpose.

I sense a joyful expectation and some excitement as we wander along the path laid through the landscape. Large open spaces with some eagles circling high above our heads, mountains, some with snow on top and some with waterfalls, valleys with cosy villages here and there, hills with changing vegetation, roaring rivers with jumping salmon, gurgling creeks with whirring insects, lots of colours, light and fragrances. You might think we don't want to walk through the whole magnificent landscape. It will take many days and be exhausting. However, that is not the case. First, there is no time here, as we are here as consciousness. Second, imagine that we are hovering or gliding through the landscape and can instantly move from one place to another. It is like moving in a dream.

The happy anticipation changes to an impatience in Jacor, and we are rapidly approaching the place where Janir and I must let him continue without us, namely the Flower Bridge. From here it looks like a bridge made of flowers in every imaginable colour. A breath-taking sight. As we come closer, we see that the bridge is a flickering energy field. Now Jacor is half a step ahead of us, but still with me on his left side and Janir on his right. We stop and Jacor turns to us. He is one big smile, happy as a young child. There is no thought, no sense and the only feeling is happiness in the unconditional love for everything. We let this feeling move between us until Jacor turns towards the bridge and begins the journey over it. He does not look back. It is as if he has forgotten us. Not negative. His focus is now on what he is longing for. Janir and I remain standing by the bridge awhile before we move towards the external consciousness of the world.

After Jacor's wish, his body is not embalmed, but after three days cremated and the ashes scattered into the sea to enter the planetary cycle as soon as possible. There is a short ceremony to honour the body and the planet, but not Jacor. The body is not him.

The following days we can sense Jacor's presence. Not as a yearning or a sorrow, but as a sign that the consciousness behind Jacor tells us that all is well.

The other people

After Jacor's transition, and because of my talks with Memton, I feel I have come closer to Janir. One morning, so early that it is still cold in my study, Janir comes to visit, announced by Cantor. She looks serious, but not as if there is something alarming. I cannot quite decipher it.

We sit down in front of each other and she says, "I have spoken to Memton, and we have decided that I must share some deep secrets I bear with you."

I must look like one question mark, for she continues, "Yes, I am also one of the initiates who, just like Memton, is a bearer of wisdom."

There is a short pause while I recall what I know about Janir. She knows a lot, especially about nature, but I never had the impression she knew forbidden wisdom. By forbidden wisdom I mean wisdom that should not be shared with the uninitiated.

"Yes," I say without being able to shape additional sentences that describe the many emotions and thoughts that swirl in my consciousness.

Janir continues, "You lack an overall picture of human history from the beginning of this planet, and I have that knowledge. This is necessary for you, otherwise the knowledge you have gathered so far will fly around like little pieces without an anchor point. This means that over time it will be segmented, falling apart, and the pieces will then attach to less valuable ideas in the common consciousness."

"That sounds sensible, since we all affect and are affected by the common consciousness," I say thoughtfully.

"Memton has given you information about consciousness. Therefore, you know we are consciousness, souls, and not human beings. However, we are souls who have chosen to incarnate, experience and evolve through the human body and the physical life."

Janir becomes silent and stares into nothingness for a while. I do not feel I should ask questions or do anything else, so I wait for her to continue.

After a short while she breaks the silence and smiles at me.

"I had to figure out what and how to present it for you, but now I think we can move on.

"At the start of human evolution here on Earth, many different bodies were created in which to incarnate. Initially, these bodies were less compact, and it was easy to bring the soul into them. Slowly, as we become affected by the planet's compact physics and life on Earth in general, our bodies became heavier. This heaviness draws us further away from the knowledge that we are consciousness and not personalities in physical bodies."

"You are talking about human evolution on Earth. Are there, or have there been, other human evolutions elsewhere?" I ask.

"Yes, this is the fifth evolution in this universe, but that is not relevant and beyond what I have chosen

to speak of. It may come later. Let me now continue."

"Yes, of course. Sorry."

I reach for the jug with juice. Janir nods as I move
the jug towards her glass. I pour for both of us.

"At some point there were twenty-three human species. Not races as we know today, but species. As a
result of interference from the place in the universe
where our previous evolution was completed, one
human species, which received codes of this evolution, was selected to advance evolutionary opportunities. Against nature's general law of evolution,
today we are only one physical human species of
significance, although this species contains many
races, which are best known by different skin tones
and body shape, although other things are different as well.

"Another human species has chosen a non-physical evolution, focusing on other things. We inhabit
the same planet and basically the same places, but
Shee, which I will call them, have their consciousness in a different frequency band, and are therefore not visible to the physical, human race. You
may say that we are brothers and sisters, because
we, as consciousness, come from the same place,
even consciousness does not have a place. At the
beginning, in the less physical state, we lived side
by side, but, as our species became more and more
focused in the physical, our sense of the Shee, who
kept their lightness, disappeared when they opt-
ed out of life in a physical body. Shee's bodies re-
mained ethereal. Shee withdrew from their phys-

ical brothers and sisters, as these were, in every way, very 'heavy' and 'brute'. This heavy and brute is not wrong. It is part of experiencing the physical evolution. I hope that at some point the Shee and us can live together for the better of the planet, and take advantage of each other's wisdom of life, drawn from the many lives in physical and non-physical incarnations respectively. I may add that this is the fifth time that life has started all over on this planet. This happened so that life could get the best opportunities for success."

What Janir tells literally opens a new dimension in my understanding of life and its evolution. I understand that life has "started up" several times, here on the planet, and consciousness, us, has undergone evolution somewhere else in the universe. I am curious if I will experience something from lives elsewhere, other than here on the planet, in my non-physical journeys.

I look down into the jug, but we are out of fruit juice. Cantor is apparently out on one of his many errands, so I suggest to Janir that we take a break.

"It's a great idea. It is hard for me to be so mental for so long and you need time to get a grip on what I've filled your head with. Let's go for a walk and see if we can find any juice or maybe fruit. It will be great."

On our walk in the near vicinity of the temple, we get hold of dates, figs, bananas and a pineapple. In addition, I fill the jug with mixed fruit juices. We will also need cold water, but we have plenty of this in the temple. You just have to ask for it to be brought up from the well facility under the temple. I have deliberately chosen not to have a service agreement on water delivery because I am distracted in my work by the deliveries that show up all the time to check whether the jugs are to be filled.

While we walk in the heat of noon, I promise myself that I will go to the bath house this evening, where I can wash off all sweat and dust and then finish with a cool bath, so it is easier to fall asleep. I have a bathtub, but tonight it will be the bath house.

Most of the walk takes place in silence. I experience a great peace being with Janir. It becomes natural for me to enjoy being in the moment and take in life as it may come. To relax in life, you may say. At this moment, I get the idea it is probably how I should live. Oh, the stupid word—"should"—too often appears in my thoughts and is the root of a bad conscience.

We arrive back at the temple. Cantor is back as well and I ask him to sort out the fruit and send bids for some water. We take the fruit juice into the study. I decide to tell Janir about the being of nature who, after many considerations, chose to incarnate as a human being. It must be mentioned that natural creatures are not the same as creatures in nature, such as animals and insects.

I have just finished my tale when Cantor comes with the fruit and the water. When he has left us again, Janir begins, "I'll try to give you a simple picture of this complex subject. To do so, I must repeat some of what has probably already been told you by Memton. You must bear with that.

"Just as humans are incarnate consciousness, natural beings are also consciousness living on Earth. Natural beings do not need a body, but have an ability to take shape after the old species before the uniformity. They are supporters of mankind and have the task of ensuring that nature can assist the human being in its life on Earth. There are two different groups of consciousness: consciousness embodied as human beings, and consciousness of beings of nature, but living a life at a different level than humans, making sure that everything in nature works according to the laws of nature."

"Can I have been embodied as a being of nature?"

"It's not likely. It is extremely rare that beings of nature incarnate in human bodies or the other way around. Remember that this is about consciousness with specific tasks and not bodies with souls, if you see the difference. One can say it is a division of labour. Only when a natural soul can benefit from it, or have a special task, will it be right for it to become embodied as a human soul does it, namely in a human body. Remember that it is the consciousness in nature that works for the embodied, human souls.

"People who work a lot with nature or who are sensitive to these vibrations in general, can get a sense of the beings that work there. It will therefore be such people who can discover a consciousness of nature in a human body. People of nature will act differently to an ordinary human, and often take shape after the old races, before the unification, but not so different in appearance that it will make a stir.

"As nature works according to strict rules, there is a higher being that manage these rules and ensures that the beings that are closest to nature and provide the practical work follow these rules of nature. We can call them deva consciousness."

It comes to mind that I have not received an answer to a specific question.

"I must remember to ask you if the human body has a memory."

Janir replies, "Yes, definitely. There are different levels of which the body is working with the brain, for there are memory cells elsewhere in the body than in the brain. That's the way you can train to be good at certain things and react instinctively; for example, when you are sword fighting. You don't have time to think about your thrust. The body stores traumatic experiences as well."

Janir would like to move on with the things she has planned to tell me.

"I will now tell you a little about the earliest times regarding the population of the planet. The first era, which we call Mu, Lemuria, started five hundred million years ago. It is not possible to date periods precisely. Not to get it exactly, anyway. This is because time is not linear, but varies. One may say that sometimes time is slowing down and at other times, running faster. It depends on the common awareness. A high awareness causes time to move faster, while a low awareness makes time move slower."

"But a sun year is a sun year, right?"

"Yes, but the wisdom that consciousness can 'produce' varies, so one year will be perceived differently in different periods."

"I can understand this, but, on the other hand, it is illogical."

"You are right, but it is because consciousness influences the universe. One can say that the logical/mental formulas are continuously being changed by consciousness."

"Oh, I think I see it now: truth is constantly changing. Continue your story."

"In the beginning, creatures we incarnated in were hermaphrodites. They therefore had offspring without a partner. At the same time, some were as small as insects while others were huge. There were many species, and they were very different. Some looked like, for example, fish while others looked like dogs. Later there was a separation, and the species had two sexes."

"So, we started to incarnate in the animal kingdom."

"That is right, and some of the first animals were the dolphins, because it was easier to move in water, since we were not used to the physical."

"It makes perfect sense."

"Our own era, the Alt-era, started 500,000 years ago. Here we began to standardise our host bodies and we ended up with species with roughly the same appearance, ability and mental capacity. The work was done on the physical and the mental, but we did not understand the spirit part. Initially, there were a number of prototypes, and the DNA in the semen and egg was adjusted. Much later, other adjustments ran wild because of the lust for power, but you already know that."

"Yes, but it's great to get more pieces in place, to connect things."

Janir gets up and prepares to leave.

"This is enough for both of us today. I'm going back to my work, and you've no doubt something you need to do as well. It's great to have another to share things with, but I don't know if this knowledge will ever be used."

"Oh, we must hope. Life and humanity cannot continue in this way, guided by decadent leaders."

I bow to say goodbye and Janir is quickly out of the room.

In dialogue with nature

After Janir has told me about nature and the spirits of nature, I become aware of the largest tree outside my home. As everything in nature is subject to consciousness that follows the laws of nature and makes sure that everything is taken care of, I have made it a habit to greet the large, old tree. Often, I walk over to it and put a hand on its rough bark, to greet it in a more physical way. I do so with an appreciative approach by which I say I recognise the life of the tree and the life in me, and we both have significance. It gives me a sense of peace and harmony. Is it the tree's spirit I feel when I feel peace and harmony?

I have had problems with many ants coming into my home. To begin with there were but a few, and they did not make much trouble, but at some point there were more and it began to be too much for me. Therefore, I decide to communicate with the deva of the ants, the consciousness in charge of the ants, and in that way to make an agreement about their whereabouts in my home. I sit down in my good chair, close my eyes and contact the deva. It appears as an ant head against a white background. I greet it first and then communicate that I want the ants to stay in the garden, for example, in the stone fence close to the house. I relay I am grateful for the understanding of the deva, bow and end the meeting.

It seems that my wish has been heard. For the next few days I see no ants in my home. Eight days pass before the ants start to reappear and I must re-communicate my desire to the deva of the ants. The ants disappear subsequently and, after about eight days I once again see some ants running along the walls. It does not seem possible to make a long-term agreement with the ants, but I do not know what to do.

During the coming night I experience that the large old tree outside my house, indeed just outside my bedroom, contacts me. It brings the message: "Ask the ants to come to me, then I will take care of them." It is not conveyed with words, but that is the message I become aware of. I am very surprised. I have never heard of anyone being contacted by a tree, but of course I thank it for the offer.

When I wake up the next morning and have shaken off the faintness of the night, I contact the deva of the ants once again.

"I was contacted by the tree outside the window. It suggests that the ants in the house move out to live there, and it will take care of them. I ask you to contact the spirit of the tree, so you two can make an agreement."

I end this with a sense of reverence. It thus becomes an agreement between two deva's and not between human consciousness and a deva.

A few days pass and I see no ants in the house. When I pass the tree, I always welcome it and thank it for the help. After five days without any ants showing up, and as I come to the tree one afternoon, I discover that there is a small anthill in the grass near the trunk. I send my gratitude to the tree and welcome the fact that a lasting solution has been reached. At the same time, I am touched that a spirit of nature chose to contact me and spend time and energy helping a human being when I know that people generally do not have a great understanding of nature, even though it contributes everything we need, not just to survive, but to be able to live well.

I have also learned that agreements with nature must be maintained, perhaps once a week, and it is reasonable that agreements should be reviewed at intervals. Had I chosen to contact the deva of the ants once a week, I would probably be without ants in the house. I feel very honoured to be part of this, for most people, secret life.

After this experience I use the opportunity for communication every time I come across a bloodthirsty mosquito when I go to sleep. And it works! This is done in the following way. I contact the deva of the mosquitoes and say I will let the mosquito get one bite, for example, on the upper side of a finger, in return for getting peace from mosquitoes the rest of the night. Under no circumstances will I be bitten on the face. Then I lay my hands with the back of my hands upwards for easy access, and, in a matter of moments, I hear a buzz and feel a mosquito land on a finger. Shortly after I feel a prick and, after a little minute, I sense that mosquito take off into the darkness. I have never been disturbed after such a visit, and the next day I only see a small mosquito bite on my finger. There has never been any large swelling or itching.

My home is close to a small hill. Here, I often seek to get away from disturbing thoughts and find calm by getting a different focus. The mound is covered with grass and low vegetation, the colours of which change over the year. There is a small collection of young trees as well, some of which are fruit trees. There are also berries of various kinds throughout the year. In some places boulders protrude from the soil of the mound. Here I tend to sit with my back against the wind, sensing the surrounding landscape and the sky above me. I can open all senses so that the sounds and fragrances of nature mix in with the overall symphony. This removes my focus from everyday thought and self-created worries.

One day when I sit on the rocks at the top of the hill with my eyes closed, sensing nature around me, I hear a faint snort from behind. I open my eyes and slowly turn my head to discover a young stag standing close by, nipping the leaves of a sapling. It obviously drew my attention to the fact it was there so I would not be frightened if I suddenly discovered it. I send a "hi" in my thoughts and then turn my head away. It should be allowed to eat in peace, just as it lets me sit in peace on "my" rock. After a while it disappears between the trees. It was a nice, life-affirming experience that falls well in line with my experience with the tree, the ants and the mosquitoes.

I have become aware that I often hum a particular tune when I go to and from the hill with the boulders. It's not a familiar tune, but just something I came up with. One day I get a feeling it is a tune I hum along with the natural spirits who are around the hill, and I see it now as an invitation to a communication with these spirits.

One day I ask if there is anything I can do for them and get the answer that I, as a human being, can more easily communicate with the people's awareness in the area than they can. They would like to see something done about the many rocks that lie on the cultivated fields in the area. It seems messy, and the rocks are in the way of those who grow on the land and maintain the soil and plants. Then I sit down on the rock on the mound and send out the following message to the common consciousness: "The fields shall be cleaned up. The stones disrupt the work and harmony in the area." I hope that people pick up this thought as their own and start the process. To my great surprise, the next morning I see three men with a cart, moving across the fields and picking up the rocks. They continue all day long, only interrupted by occasional rests.

After Janir's story about the Shee, I realise that it is actually the Shee that use the tune to create a conscious connection with me. Strangely I can't remember the tune if I just want to hum it. It is only when the contact is created that it shows up in me, and at the same time I feel the love that flows between us. Often there is no mental communication, but merely a sense of cohesion and recognition of our existence. It is always wonderfully liberating to make contact, and I always feel a joy in this meeting.

Journey through the land

Here is another description of a nocturnal experience that did not feel like a dream.

It is unbearably hot and dry, bone-dry. The dust is stirred up by my quick steps on the narrow path of the open landscape. The dry, stiff grass has long forgotten that there is something called water, and I yearn unspeakably after the rainy season, while I steer towards a point in the distance where I hope will still be water.

The only thing I wear is a piece of hide that hangs down in front of my genitals. It gives some protection against the harsh vegetation I wade through on my way. I hold a stick in my left hand. For a long time there has been no game to shoot, so, since I have no more arrows, I left my bow behind but kept the string. Bow and arrows I can quickly make when I need these again. At the moment I must live on what I can dig out of the earth. It takes experience to find roots, insects and reptiles.

When I travel through the land, I follow the flow of energy. In this way The Great Mother leads me on the way. If I see a creature coming towards me on the stream, I sense whether I should give way or meet it.

Much of the country is undisturbed by people because we wander with the flow between destinations; those places that are important and that are destined for us. There are places for people, and other places we have nothing to do with and therefore we are not called upon to go there. The currents do not lead us there.

If a place has an interest, several streams meet there, and each stream contributes with its energy and therefore there is a higher energy, creating a focal point. We know then that the site has, or may have, importance. At the same time, it is the people who amplify the energies at the focal points, and this increases the overall energy there.

The knowledge my people and I have comes from the sister who, in past times, sowed our consciousness on the planet. We connect to the planet's consciousness as the living creature she is.

Slowly, I slip out of the meditative state while trying not to think. I am consciousness, not thought.

I was far back in time. I thought humans and animals followed the paths, but I now know the paths were created by those who followed the energy streams that cross the landscape. Later, this knowledge was lost, apparently like so much else. I feel that life is connected to the Earth. It is the Earth that is common to all life. This is where the energy for physical life has its starting point.

The broken heart

Still with a sense of great contact to the Earth, I once again slip into the darkness of sleep and am soon engrossed in yet another experience.

I am a woman sitting next to my husband who is lying on the couch in a rocky cave up in the mountains. Both he and I have a very dark complexion. He is badly injured after a fall in this mountainous country and has many internal injuries. He was hunting for mountain goats and, on his way back to the cave with a goat on his back, he had stepped on a loose rock. Fortunately, it happened close to the cave, so I could help him back here. The cave smells of moist rock, smoke and fur.

The couch of rock is a platform at the back of the cave. A recess is made and then filled with fur. This creates a soft bed, and the recess makes sure that fur and people do not easily fall on the rock floor.

I am deeply frustrated and almost in shock. I give him some tonic herb decoction, nurture his exterior wounds and sit now on a fur on the floor next to him and hold his hand. He tries to smile, but it becomes a grimace. He has severe pain and is slightly foggy. He slowly slips away in a restless sleep and I can no longer stand being in the cave.

I release his hand and walk outside. Here is a large ledge covered with sand, rocks and boulders. It is still very hot outside the cave although the sun will soon set. The heat is now reflected from the dusty rocks at the top of the plateau where the entrance to the cave is. I move a little way from the entrance of the cave and walk closer to the edge. Far below, and as far as the eye can see, is a desert with a mixture of low mountains, rocks and sand. A dreary place to settle, but life does not always form the way one desires or expects. For now there are good hunting opportunities, so there is no need to move on.

I love him unspeakably, and it physically hurts in my heart when I think I will soon lose him and stand alone in this barren region.

I am not distraught about coping with this life on my own, but having to live without him will be unbearable. I get crazy thinking about it, and, as it hurts terribly in the chest and abdomen, emotions are even more difficult to handle.

What is left of me, of my life, when my love and all I live and breathe for will be torn away? Can I live with a broken heart? Yes, a heart that in a way has been torn out of my chest?

I crouch with my arms folded around my knees and my forehead on my arms. Tears draws lines in the dust on my forearms, and my legs have become numb. I must return and see how he is doing.

He is awake, even though his eyes are closed. I can hear it in his breathing. Again I sit next to the bed and bring him the bowl with water. He can neither hold the bowl nor lift his head, and most of the water ends up on his chest or runs down both sides of his strong neck. I get up again, take the bowl and fill it only half from the water jar. By gently lifting his head a bit, I can pour some water into his mouth.

He shrinks and begins to cough. "No more water," he splutters while his face shows great pain.

No, no more water. It only prolongs his agony. With his hand in mine, I lie beside him on the furs and slowly he relaxes. Now he opens his eyes a bit and I hold his gaze while he whispers to me.

"You must live for both of us. I will soon give my body back to Uma."

He breathes in to have air for another sentence.

"No, my beloved, I do not understand life, but there is a time when one is born of the Mother through one's human mother and you walk on the Mother until she senses it is appropriate to call the borrowed body back. I move towards the stars and we will meet when the Mother once again takes your body back. The treasure will be the day when we re-unite.

"Now let's be together and close to the Mother," I say, and turn my body on the side next to him on the bed with my arm cautiously around him.

We both cry quietly and I can feel that the Mother's love is very present. I start to relax and his breathing is also calm. I turn my attention briefly to the Mother and thank her that I have met and lived with this man.

Now all becomes completely silent. He no longer breathes but has taken towards the stars.

The last stone is laid on the grave and I am sick; literally. While I dragged the stones and made a barrow over him, I had planned to spend the night in the cave and then be on my way the next morning. But now that I sit with my back against a cliff, I cannot stand the idea that tomorrow I will walk out of the cave and see the stone heap which is not usually lying there, stretching towards the sky. I must collect what is most needed and leave in the night and sleep where I fall by fatigue.

As I tumble through the night with the moon as my only companion, the last hours are clear in my mind. He was washed and laid on a hide lying on the floor. With the last ochre I painted the Mother on his body, and then I used the hide to pull him out to the little recess I had managed to scrape in the hard surface, near the entrance of the cave. After placing him in the recess, still lying on the hide, I put his bow and quiver with arrows, the spear and his bowl, which I stuffed with berries. Finally, I tucked the hide around him, so the stones would not touch him directly.

The work with the stones took place in a stupor of exhaustion and despair. His body had been crushed, but so had mine; not physically, but by sorrow, and the pain was unbearable.

Gradually, the images slide into the back of my mind and are replaced by the sound of my beating heart, as if it wants to escape from its captivity in my chest and run away and hide, never again to be found.

I wake as Yadar, covered in sweat, and feel both exhausted, very thirsty and with a horrible feeling I am being driven insane by the emotion and intensity of the dream. The least part of the experience is that I was a woman in the dream.

I rise from my bed, put on my loincloth and walk outside. The coolness of the night makes me feel better and, with the help of some deep breaths, I gradually calm again, even though the dream is still lurking in my mind and body.

Thoughts about the dream slowly rise to the surface.

"I must not see myself as a man, but as a human being who, in this life, acts as a man in a man's body. It's like wearing an advanced costume, which at the same time leads me to feel like a man and act as such. If in some lives I act as a woman and in others as a man, am I neither the one nor the other? Is it just a mask I wear? And in that case, what am I? Consciousness."

It gets too cold to stand outside, so I walk inside and drink a nice amount of water. The cold and the water gives me the urge to urinate, which I do before I lie on the bed. With a sheet above me, I lie on my back and stare up at the ceiling, but soon I slip into sleep again.

The chief's son

Another dream is pushing itself into the emptiness of my sleep, and I have a strange feeling that I am still on the same continent as in the previous dream. I am again a woman and, as I look down at myself, my skin is completely dark and I merge with the shadows in the hut.

We have been best friends since our earliest childhood. Now that she is to marry the young chieftain, I can see that it is not just because of a tradition that they have to be together. It cannot be any other way. The same night, as the wedding ceremony took place, I dreamed of two stars who met in the sky, fused and became one larger and brighter star.

As she gives birth to her first child, a boy, I see in a daydream in a quiet moment in the middle of the day: the child grows up and becomes a good and well-liked leader, like his father, and wise and empathic, like his mother, with good contact to nature. He is a blessing to the tribe. When I look into the opportunities of the future, he gives us the longest life as a tribe.

In the dream I focus on the boy and suddenly I am sucked into the child, and I sense that I am now the child, but now I am an adult. It is night and I stand and sense a very intense atmosphere, a close connection to my parents and ancestors. It is as if the connection runs through all generations and ends up in the earth where I stand. Yes, more than that, I am connected with the Mother herself, with the origins of life, the circle and the spiral.

I stand here and think back over my life until this time, when I have just become chief after my dear father. I gaze towards the mountains in the distance and forget the clan that dances around me.

I chose my parents with great care. My father, who was a young chief for a small tribe when I was born, is not to be described as wise, but he was just and well-liked and was a good leader. My mother, on the other hand, had an incredible empathy when it came to people and nature, and she was an indispensable supporter of my father, both as his wife and in his role as chief. Many wise words flowed from her to him. My mother is wise, but her wisdom is used in the quiet. She had no need to move forward. She tells me that I was born almost without pain, and that she herself attended my birth dance.

I remember when I was to receive my hunting spear, which inaugurated me as an adult hunter in the tribe. I was very young. I see as I look back. I was standing, scouting for the hunting group that was to initiate me. I was alone in ritual space and felt very nervous about what was to come. After this I would no longer be looked upon as a child with an adult's indulgence. Now it was serious.

When the hunters dance around me, I try to find the emotions of being important and worthy of later becoming chief, but these powerful feelings are absent. The emotions I feel are more that I am revered as the son of the chieftain rather than for who I am.

In the next few years I show my qualities and I feel

that I am gradually being seen for who I am and what I can become.

My father dies unexpectedly before he reaches old age. It is then my mother who hands over the spear and the lion hide in the ceremony during which I take over my father's position and responsibilities.

I feel proud and honoured as all the warriors dance around me. I have finally become chief as it had always been determined. But suddenly the emotions and posture change. The expression the tribe sees on my face they interpret as a sense of significance. But if they could feel what I feel, it would be almost petrified horror at the fact that everything is now resting on my shoulders. Suddenly it is up to me. I have a huge responsibility for the tribe and its survival in an uncertain future.

Of course, I have the medicine man, but he is just an old fool, a master of ceremonies who refuses to die. I feel a great thankfulness for still having a wise woman as my mom.

That I started as a woman in this dream and then become a man confuses me. Can I be born in several bodies at the same time, or is it more like information for me about the boy's past?

"I chose my parents with great care?" I must have been conscious before I was born. Yes, before I was conceived. And one can make choices about the next life if you are conscious.

The king's dancer and musician

I have taken a nap late in the afternoon and it gives me a wonderful experience.

It starts at night when I am standing outside, looking up at the constellation Orion. Then I move closer and closer and can eventually only see the three stars in the belt. I don't know if it really is me coming to the stars, or it's the stars coming to me.

The light from the stars is getting weaker, and now I can see that they are placed over three four-sided pyramids. To the left of the pyramids lies a gigantic lion, formed in the rock. I turn my head and follow its gaze. It looks up at the constellation Leo. Very appropriate, although I do not in any way become wiser.

Now it gets brighter around me. First, I think that it is sunrise, but then I see that I am in a beautifully decorated room with a lot of equipment and clothes. I am together with some beautifully dressed women. Some are dancers and others have musical instruments. I look down at my body and discover that I am a woman myself, equally beautifully dressed and with a tambourine in my hand. I now know that I am a dancer and musician in the Per'aa, the Great House, the royal palace.

We are all ready and stand at a wide, closed door. A servant opens the door from the outside and peeks in. He whispers with the master of ceremonies, who now looks startled. The servant leaves and the master of ceremonies turns to us. "The king will greet you personally and is on his way."

We become troubled, but receive strict orders to act as professionals. Now the door swings open and the king enters in all his splendour. I stand in the front and am surprised to see that it is a beautiful young woman who enters. Now I remember. Her name is Hatshepsut. Earlier she was a queen, but chose to be king, not to stand as weak and less qualified for the throne. We all love her.

Hatshepsut walks around to us all and we are all deeply touched by the visit.

Hatshepsut approaches me and I cannot look down. She smiles and looks me straight in the eyes. We must present ourselves.

"Your Royal Highness. Gamila." I curtsy.

"Beautiful. Stand by your strength and your femininity."

I get tears in my eyes and look down. "Thank you."

Hatshepsut lifts my chin and looks in my eyes once again. "And keep your head high!"

She still smiles and moves to the next. I curtsy again and gently dab the tears away with a scarf that one of the girls hands me. It was a great experience and I can still feel her touch under my chin and her scent in my nose.

Before I slip away, I get a feeling that although our lives are strictly governed, my life in the palace is good compared to that of most outside.

The dying warrior

I lie on my back with eyes closed. I feel a terrible pain in my abdomen and left thigh. It feels as if I don't have long to live, and, even with my eyes closed, it feels as if the bed is spinning. My arms are down along my sides, and I can feel that the bed is made of fur. I hear a bonfire and smell incense. A woman begins to sing and I open my eyes. I find myself in a small round hut with rafters clad with clay. There is a smoke hole at the top of the roof. It is my woman, Nascha, who sings.

It all starts to come back. I had been struck by two arrows and woke up for a moment and discovered that I was being carried on a hide stretcher with my head first and my legs dangling down the rear. No word was spoken, and I heard only the breath of the bearers and the hissing sound as they penetrated the tall grass.

My wounds sting awfully, and now I smell the ointment that the wounds were smeared with before they were dressed. I try to call Nascha, but I only bring forth a grunt. I can barely breathe. She turns and comes to the bed. She sits down on the edge and takes my hand. We look at each other.

"Mato will come later. There are many injured."

I nod. I know Nascha is talking about the medicine man. I want to speak, but can only think, "Yes, it was very violent. Fear. Panic."

There is no need to talk anymore. We live with death every day and we know what will happen when I have gone to the land of the ancestors. She will be dependent on my family, primarily my brethren, until she finds herself a new man. The children follow her.

She has tears in her eyes and continues her song. She raises her voice, as much to give herself strength as to help me. I feel the strength of the voice, the melody and the words. My eyes close and I feel calm. I am proud of her and I know she will manage. She has many skills and much courage.

It is dim in the hut, but now I sense that the hide is pulled from the entrance and the light pours in. It penetrates my eyelids. It must be the medicine man. All pain is gone. There is no more heaviness and stiffness in my body. He greets me and smiles. I see the smile through my closed eyelids. I stand in a white smoke and sense figures approaching. I am home!

The guiding star

It is noon and I sit in meditation in my cubicle in the temple. I sit cross-legged on a padded stool that inclines slightly downwards in front with a low table at the same height as the stool. On the table two lamps burn, and between them stands a jar of sand, intended for incense sticks, but I do not feel like using fragrances for this meditation. There is a jug with water as well and my personal mug. Early in the morning I decided what I want to do with this meditation. After being stuck in my studies, I will try to connect with one of my potential futures. Perhaps I can bring back something that can be used in my scientific work.

I close my eyes, and after a few deep breaths the thoughts subsides, and it gets dark for my inner vision. Slowly the darkness acquires a tone of blue, and gradually there are shining points on the dark blue background. Ah, the night sky. I have been studying the night sky too much lately. I shake my head slightly to get rid of the picture.

It is dark again, but shortly the night sky with its stars comes back for my inner sight.

"Hmm, it is apparently not a vision from the future this time, but what can you tell me?" I ask the picture.

I start to look at the stars' locations. Can I recognise some constellations, or is it a purely fantasy image of a sky?

Well, here's a constellation that I know. It can be

nothing but the lion.

The picture is slightly distorted compared to what I know, but I just note this and wait for a message to come through, because the picture does not immediately give me any new information.

Suddenly one of the stars brightens; one that I have not first noticed. I fully focus on the phenomenon. "What is it? What is this?" I ask. "What do I see?" I grow frustrated and pull things out of my memory to see if any of it fits what I see. "Oh, damn!" The star suddenly slips down below the horizon and disappears, and the sky is completely empty of stars even though it remains dark blue. I did not get anything out of it. "Damn," I think again. "Why am I always so sluggish?!" I take a deep breath. This cannot be true. I must be able to get something out of this vision. I relax and slip out of my mental spin. "Yes, of course. I shouldn't think, but feel!"

After another deep breath I open for all impressions. The star now returns to the sky, but this time significantly higher up. "What can it mean?" I try to concentrate on the light, but I feel that I must lower my inner gaze. When my focus reaches the ground, which appears as a black silhouette against the dark blue, my gaze is allowed to rest. There is a hill. No, it's a house. I feel that it is my home. Suddenly the house comes rushing towards me, and the scene changes to a warm, sunny day. I see myself as a boy of about eight years, standing and looking up into the sky. The star is clear to see even though the sun shines. I get the feeling that the star is standing still while the sun is moving. A beacon that can be used day and night; a guiding star. I notice that this is the future, a possible future. The boy turns his head and looks to the left. I now see through his eyes, which are also mine. Something has been drawn on the gable. I myself have drawn it. It is a stylistic image that I do not see clearly, but I sense a great love and the word Jamaya. A name. A girl. I sense that my face wears a blissful expression. I'm in love!

Now the scene changes and completely different emotions are in play. They are certainly not pleasant and I know them so well. I shift perspective and become one with the story. I am a young man while I remain an observer.

He had chosen the break between them. Not because he wanted to leave Jamaya. On the contrary, he had never felt more connected with another human being. But because the mission he was selected for would separate them physically for the rest of this life.

Here, far from the pyramids, whose tops pointed to the sky and whose shadows, at the same time, pointed to the Earth—in itself a symbol of two directions—they had to be separated. He had broken bonds earlier in his life, but this was the hardest thing.

There were not many days when the silence descended on the quarry, but today it was quiet, and the only movement was the dust that was whirled high up by the wind. He thought of his dear teacher, Imhotep, who had prepared him for the journey and who had always known about it.

He must go and assist the long-awaited prophet,

Yeshua from the house of Sananda, in his work to spread the crystal energy. He himself would contribute with the brightest Atlantic energy, and others would take part in the work as well.

Jamaya's face was marked by her emotional pain and her tears, but behind them he caught a glimpse of the light and the smile that had always given him the courage and the power to live. He would always hold both the light and the smile in his heart.

No audible word was heard during their last meeting. Jamaya understood that it was he who must fulfil this assignment. There were also the emotional pictures she saw when she looked into her future. There was always a long shadow that reached her, and at the other end of the shadow was the silhouette of a man, so far away that he could barely be discerned.

I am deeply moved as I come back from this experience. What can or should I use it for? Or should it be used? When in history does this happen? It is not in this life. The boy and the man are the same and I'm them. I did not live in such a house as a child, or have a childhood girlfriend and later a woman like Jamaya. And I have not experienced the star that could be seen in full sunlight, or encountered records of such an incident. I am convinced, however, that this is a possibility for the future.

I give more thought to the experience. If the young man, meaning myself, had such a profound connection with Jamaya, my mission had to be of utmost importance, which I also felt during the experience. While I am still in my expanded state of consciousness, I wonder why Jamaya cannot simply go with him, and I receive the answer that it is necessary for the man to devote himself entirely to the work that has to be done. It is no use for him to be distracted from carrying out his mission.

I try to stay open, but there is no more information. With a few deep breaths I let go of the desire to know more. After sitting for a few minutes, I turn off the two lights on the small table in front of me and walk out into the hallway and continue to the common room. The experience follows me for a long time this day. Only when I get home and start various practical things does the event move into the background.

As I sit at home in the evening writing about the events of the day, I try to get a little structure into the things I have learned.

I have the constellation, the lion. It's slightly distorted, but that's probably less important. Then there is the star that lights up strongly, after which it quickly disappears beneath the horizon to resurface again later. I also have the information that the star stands still while the sun continues its journey across the sky.

A few years pass, and the boy has become a man with a good education. I do not see Jamaya's importance , but the young man must embark on an important mission to a prophet called Yeshua. The mission has also been known for a long time. The place doesn't look like anything I know, although I know that the man should use a crystal energy from here, being Alt. This energy clears our thoughts and gives us a greater sense of what is happening around us.

Although I feel that I now have some possible answers, these lead to new questions: What connection is there between the star, the boy, the man and the prophet, and what should the prophet do with the clearing energy? These are the questions that I will move on with at the earliest opportunity.

In the afternoon I sit and think of Jamaya. She brings many strong feelings forward when she appears in the dreams, but is there a message in this? I slowly fade away from the daytime consciousness and a red light comes to me.

A red planet and a princess in red

With mixed emotions such as powerlessness, sadness and anger, she slides through the colonnades of a palace, where everything emits a muted, red tinge. Her dress, which is red as well, reaches almost to the floor. Her hair, however, is black. There is a faint sound of air moving, but I don't know whether it is her gliding motion through the broad colonnade, or a breeze that creates the sound when it nestles past the pillars.

She has said goodbye, but at a distance. She could not bear to see him so shortly before she has to lose him. The starship has left the planet to take him on this important diplomatic mission. She has really tried, but there came no better solution. He was born to take on this mission. This was about much more than just the two of them and what they had together. In the beginning, she was in despair, for she needed him here. How else would she manage? She knew her own strength, but it had left her. Tears run down her cheeks as she senses that he thinks of her. Her power returns and she knows they will meet again. Maybe not in this life, but then in another. Now she knows that she can take everything that life places in front of her, for their reunion is waiting out there somewhere.

While I slowly drift out of the dream, I have a distinct feeling that it is me who travels away in the starship, and it is my beloved I leave in the palace. The scene takes place in a star system far from Earth. It is a parallel to the way Jamaya and I parted in Egypt in another vision.

May we meet the same consciousness we have encountered in other lives? Are there some bonds of consciousness that go beyond the individual life that allow us to recognise each other without knowing it through these strong emotions? Strong because they are strengthened through these many meetings, life after life? Yes, maybe even between lives. Why not?

Yeshua

I move forward in the event with the guiding star in a dream that night. I dream, but at the same time I feel very alert and attentive, as during the meditation earlier today. It starts a little confusingly: Clear water flowing, in two streams, over the edge of a large and beautiful fountain formed like petals on a flower. Halfway down, one stream turns black while the other turns white, but when the black and white liquid join in a larger basin around the fountain, the liquid becomes crystal clear and I feel a great love. I don't know what it means, but the sense of love and a sense of clarity are not to be mistaken.

The dream changes, and I now experience being the young man from the meditation in the temple earlier today.

Imhotep comes to me hastily for a meeting outside the city walls. We meet here at midday, where the sand burns through my sandals and the sun penetrates through the palm leaves, so that no one will see my departure, because no one is out here. I do not fully understand this secrecy, but I trust my teacher. In the temple he has a different name, but deep down I know that it is Imhotep, even though he lived many hundreds of years ago with this name.

In a brief glimpse I get a picture of a father who puts his hand on his son's head. It is the father, Ptah, and his son Imhotep. I see the name of the father written in glyphs next to the son's name, which contains the same glyphs, just backwards and with an extra glyph, an owl. Words such as wisdom and clear sight come to me.

Imhotep gives me instructions.

"Follow Yeshua the anointed from the house of the lion and support the process with your clear energy. There are dark forces that do not want the light to be brought to mankind. The light that illuminates them, so they see that they are also the divine consciousness, the consciousness that causes them to refuse to submit to anyone or anything. The true freedom."

Imhotep holds my hands, and a great love flows between us. I know that his consciousness will always be with me, every step I take, and in every breath as well. I get the idea that he is my guiding star.

Here, the guiding star comes right into the dream. "It must mean something," I think as an observer in the dream.

I walk down to the river where a small sailboat with one man is ready to take me and my few possessions out to the estuary, to the city of Alexandria. The movements of the boat soon rock me to sleep as I lie in its bow and gaze at the sky above me.

Now I experience a dream in my dream! It is short but filled with joy and love.

A happy time

I lie in the bow of the boat with my head over the side, watching the spray of water hit the calm surface further out when the boat cuts through the water. The Nile is calm today, and we are sailing down the wide river with good speed. I feel joy and tranquillity. Is it the same sentiment as the Nile feels? Is this not my personal feeling, but a feeling that I share with all life around me? I'm calm and the Nile is calm. We rejoice in life and the existence of life.

Now I focus on the mirror image on the water's surface. A simple small cloud reflects its belly while it slowly changes shape. This picture is now disturbed by a flock of birds that, up high, is passing between the cloud and the surface of the water. The papyrus reflects its fine feathers that always move, while the olive trees appear as the peripheral background. Now I see my own face down there, a little out of place in all that nature, I think. But then her beautiful face appears close to mine. Her hair is moved by the breeze like the papyrus, and her presence comes into focus. Her warm belly against my loin, her hand on my shoulder and her scent. My joy and tranquillity shift to a euphoric happiness of existing and being able to share my life with this wonderful being.

She catches my gaze in the water and smiles. She shares my feelings. Her hand finds mine and we are simply together. What more can we expect from life other than feeling joy and love for everything that exists?

Is it Jamaya who shows up yet again, or are they just the same emotions that are called forth? Feelings like joy, happiness and love.

Yeshua – part two

The dream changes back to the young man who is on his way to support Yeshua in his energy work.

I must hand in a few letters at a particular academy in Alexandria. This annoys me as Alexandria is a detour. However, it is important that the letters do not appear in the wrong hands. The next day past noon I am in Alexandria and find the academy by the harbour, close to the large library.

Here, it is as if nothing works and everything, even time, is stretched indefinitely. Finally, the letters are delivered to the right person. Now I must find a place to stay overnight because no ships leave this late. When I leave the building, I come across a young woman who makes such an impression on me that I am suddenly in no rush to move on. Her name is Mariamne and she has had different things to do here. As I tell her that I am looking for a place to sleep, she recommends the hostel where she herself will stay overnight. We walk together to the hostel by the harbour.

As I am on my bed, I have the feeling that it is not by chance that I met Mariamne and that the troubles at the academy had delayed me just enough that the meeting was made possible.

The next morning, I am up early to get a seat on

a ship. Soon I once again sit in the bow of a ship, daydreaming.

It is night, and I recognise the star from the previous experience. As I look towards the ground again, I discover that a young man stands beneath the star and looks up at it. I sense that it is the man that I must assist. The star radiates strongly over Yeshua's head, but shortly after it turns into a burning cross.

Suddenly, I am alone with the star in the night sky and a ring has formed around it. I feel that time is somehow beginning here. Or that it is an important point in time.

It is very strange to me, being Yadar, to experience these different levels of dreams. I move between different consciousnesses and experience these as both an actor and an observer at the same time.

Now I'm back as the young man who, after a long voyage and then a trip with a caravan, finally stands in front of Yeshua's parents. Here I experience the same strong sense of love. They present themselves as Marit and Yosef and ask me to come inside.

I sense that I can tell them why I am here, and Marit tells a little about their son.

"Yeshua was about nineteen when he was married. We arranged the marriage with her family. She was from another fine family. They were married for some years, but she died at a young age. Yeshua was seized by a deep sorrow leading to a depression, and he left us, saying he had to 'find the meaning of life and what love is.' He has not yet returned, but I feel he is not far away."

I am allowed to stay overnight. As I lie down to rest, I consider my situation. Yeshua is not here, but since Imhotep has sent me here, it must be the right time.

Yosef is a stonemason, and the next morning I am awakened by the sound of metal against a rock. Still drowsy, I move outside.

"It's the next best way to get the morning cold and stiffness out of your body," he says, with a smirk. Although he is of noble descent, he has a craft.

There arises some disturbance in the picture as if something will break into this time from a different time. Fragments or pictures of Josef as a carpenter … his hammer and chisel turn into a mallet and a wood chisel, and the stone turns into wood. A clear, cool breeze comes in and the carpenter Josef disappears, while Yosef the stonemason once again stands in the bright sunshine. He lays hammer and chisel on the stone which he is going to work into a bone chest, stands upright and smiles as he wipes his forehead with the back of his hand. I walk over to help him get the stone under the lean-to so he can stand in the shadows now that the sun has become warmer.

Marit comes out of the house and gazes out through the gate. She has tears in her eyes. I can't take my eyes away from her, not even to look where her gaze rests.

Yeshua comes through the gate and is one big smile as he sees his mother. She gets a big hug, and then he notices his father under the lean-to. Yosef also gets a warm hug. Then Yeshua's eye finds me.

"And you have just come from Egypt."

It sounds like a statement, and then I am hugged too; and a powerful hug I must say. He smells as if he had plenty to drink the day before. We withdraw to the shade and Yeshua tells that he has travelled far off in the region: the Middle East, India, Egypt and parts of Europe. Here he has visited masters and religious orders and studied religions.

"I have learned the simplicity and mysteries of the world, some of which are taught in the mystery schools of Alexandria."

"I have not come across you in Egypt," I venture.

"No, you haven't heard of me or seen me. The time was not right for us to meet."

After this brief encounter with Yeshua, I come to the surface and am again on my bed, home by myself as Yadar. I get up and drink some water. Now I must write my experiences before the details slip out of my mind.

The composite Yeshua

I have spent some time making notes and feel dead tired. There is not long till morning, but I will try to connect myself to Yeshua to learn more about the crystal energy. I sit on my stool and think of the young man that I have met.

Shortly after, Yeshua shows up and greets me. Then I discover that there are more faces behind him, and soon there are thousands of them. However, they have no contours. He senses my question and explains.

"I am not a soul with creating abilities like the majority, but a soul composed of many consciousnesses or souls for a special assignment. We have gathered the characteristics of many to create the best opportunities for the crystal energy. The reason I can meet you here is that your soul is part of this awareness."

"I am very curious to know whether this special constellation worked," I say enquiringly.

Yeshua smiles a little indulgently and starts to tell.

"It was not at all as we had hoped for or figured. Our primary message was: I am like you, you are like me. I am the son of god and so are you and we are spirit."

Yeshua continues his tale.

"Through example, I show what a divine human is, but the masses only focus on the divine and exalt me to be divine and forget to elevate themselves.

Others call me a cheat. People cannot get beyond their paramount focus on god. God as the Almighty and the human being as the insignificant. We could hardly budge them from this picture. Mankind was not ready to receive this message, namely that they were so much more. But it was not in vain, for it had to start somewhere; it would not come by itself. However, we have experience from previous works. The seed was to be sown and watered. In light of earlier planetary developments, a gentler introduction of crystal energy will be preferable. Next time, the vast majority of people who are ready to receive the message will be individuals, and not large groups. We will work from 'within', and you will be one of these workers, or at least an incarnation of your soul."

I get the feeling of "well, that is all for now" from Yeshua, and Yeshua's face and all the faces behind quickly fade away. My consciousness is back in my body sitting on the stool. I haven't brought any water to the stool, so I fetch some and start to write notes.

My soul is part of the composite Yeshua. It is also in the young man who is together with the physical Yeshua and will also be incarnated in a person at another time working with the crystal energy. This shows that time is a very loose concept.

Imhotep

I stay very much in the temple at this time. Through Janir I am connected to a very secret project in which we are working to recreate a hermaphrodite being, just like those we incarnated in, long before the species was divided into two sexes, and later again when the races were made very similar. For me, however, it becomes an almost insoluble task, since the gender is already determined at conception so the offspring becomes either a male or a female. One gender will suppress the other. We must change this either-or to both.

I do not want to elaborate on this work, but would like to tell you about the person, Imhotep, whom I encountered on one of my journeys a short time ago. Like Yeshua, he is from my future, but I sense that the soul behind the person also has a connection to my own time, the Alt-era.

I am in my room in the temple when I contact Imhotep. I use the memory of our first meeting to get connected. Imhotep shows up in the same shape and attire as when the young man met him, and I experience the same emotions as I had when I appeared as the young man in the dream: a teacher, a father figure, and something much deeper, which I cannot put into words.

Imhotep greets me.

"We have always known each other, so these emotions also permeate your human consciousness."

I welcome Imhotep and am ready with my question.

"Can you tell me about the country of Egypt that the young man came from, and maybe something about the future of our civilisation?"

Imhotep begins.

"If we follow a line of my incarnations back from the time when Egypt starts to grow due to the influence of survivors from Alt, we will, after Alt's collapse, experience huge natural disasters that clean out the very chaotic and unbalanced energies on and in the planet and in common consciousness. Many people move beneath the Earth's surface, and it is only after that balancing that people from Alt emerge in many places on the planet and start new societies. We have lived apart for generations and therefore developed differently, but with many similarities. You and I are helping to create the Egypt that you met in the dream."

I think of what Jacor told about the future and Azuru Timu.

Imhotep reassures me.

"You will not experience these turbulent times in this life, and the next time you incarnate, things may have changed. It may sound strange that something is given in advance and yet not given in advance. It depends entirely on the choices that are made and on the common consciousness you are resonating with when you enter an incarnation. I strongly advise you not to focus on events which, on the one hand, will not arise in this life and, on the other hand, may not even occur in your incarnated future."

Imhotep leaves me, and I have a feeling of confidence and tranquillity concerning my immediate future.

Another diplomatic mission

I find myself in a large, dim room, so large that I cannot see the walls or the ceiling. Torches are lit around us and I have an instinctive feeling that I am not on Earth. I know that I am on a diplomatic mission.

I sit in front of the foreign warlord. There are guards farther back in the room and two a little closer to him. One of his daughters stands at his left and she has the task of serving us. It is also clear that she is placed there to appease me. She is dark haired, dressed in a long, light dress with a belt tied about her waist. She seems calmer than her father and gives the impression that she has a greater over-view and possesses more wisdom than he, who is stuck in his ideas of how everything is and how it should be.

He wants dominion over the planet, but when he attacks our countries, he finds the landscape completely deserted. We use "scorched earth tactics", but with the difference that we take everything with us, buildings, materials, animals, even plants, trees and the soils in which they live, and the water. His troops encounter only desert and no fight.

I represent the council and have full authority to act. I am calm and sense the presence of the council. He whispers something to his daughter.

I put out a remark to set the mood.

"You don't have to think about making such a good impression, so that I am good-willed when I am at home presenting this meeting to the council. I am here as a common consciousness, which means that the whole council is gathered here. I, or indeed we, can therefore make decisions here and now. I do not need to go back to the council and present anything that will then be discussed and a reaction proposed. We manage it all here."

He doesn't like to hear this. I see his insecurity, and he catches his daughter's gaze briefly to try to find something that he can hold on to. He gets her strength and love, but the rest is up to him. I sit reclining in a good chair, but lean forward and take the tin mug of tea that the daughter has put in front of me on the solid wooden table between us. It all seems rather primitive, both the interior and the clothing.

"As I see it, you only get more and more desert to rule. It amazes me that you have not considered that we can turn our tactics towards you, and instead of removing ourselves from you, turn ourselves towards your lands and leave them desolate. I can sense that your daughter has this in mind. And now that she thinks further along these lines, I see her mind darkened. Not because she is afraid for the countries and their inhabitants, but because she realises that our counterattacks will only cost the life of one person. Just think, a counterattack from us, where only one person dies!"

I could see that he caught the idea.

"It won't be possible for you to kill me. There are guards everywhere. You'll never get away from here alive."

"Dear Grand Duke, I am not here to kill you. I am a diplomat. I am here to find a solution to a serious problem for millions of people. You are like an old stubborn mule with blinkers that only follows the carrot that dangles in front of its muzzle. The mule is deaf and the eyes do not see that the carrot is withered and shrunken and is more like a corpse that hangs in gallows."

He collapses more and more in the chair, and I see that the daughter gives him her love as a fine golden thread between her heart and his.

I continue.

"I give you the opportunity now to choose to do what you most like; to find your innermost desires and live them out in the life you have yet left. What will it be? I let you free of all that has bound you, all the delusions and lies that you yourself and others have bound you in, and ask you, heart to heart, what you most want to experience."

He sighs and his gaze roams. Suddenly he appears very old. A shadow passes over his face.

I put his emotions into words.

"I see and feel the tiredness you feel. Turn this fatigue into satiety. Sated with an eventful life where you have experienced more than most and lived fully and completely; felt everything between love and hate and gathered much wisdom."

At his right side a faint, luminous outline appears. A woman fades in. He does not see her; his perception is not so high in frequency. She resembles an older version of the daughter. It's her mother. His eyes become moist. She has reached him. Love has reached him and we connect, all three, wife, daughter and envoy, to him, and layer by layer the barriers around his heart burst, like clay that dries and cracks in the sun. It all falls at his feet, becoming fine dust, almost smoke, and slips out of existence. I see his vision. A large garden or park, filled with life and colours. I sense that it was such a garden his wife loved and took care of when she was alive. He wants to find the tranquillity that the garden and the woman gave him. He wants to create peace! His gaze becomes distant, but then it stiffens and his thoughts encroach upon him as if they would crush him.

Again, I describe the scenery to him.

"I see that doubt grabs you. It's like bony fingers around your neck. Look in your daughter's eyes. Here you see both her mother, herself and the next ruler. A regent for peace, prosperity and love."

He gets up and embraces the daughter. The dark thoughts disappear and he looks into her eyes.

"My daughter, Lucia, would you take this burden from me and manage it as the next ruler?"

"Yes, Dad. But a burden it will not be as I will lift it with love."

We all have tears running down our cheeks. All has been released, the space now being filled with love. When we have all collected ourselves, the grand duke summons his secretary and dictates a short message.

"I have decided, with the help of my heart, to hand over all my duties as ruler to my daughter, Lucia. I dissolve all the ties that bind others and myself together in hatred and disagreements and will only seek peace in the last time I live."

I look at the silhouette of his former wife, and plants and trees begin to emerge in the etheric field around her. The two are manifesting the garden of calm where the resigned ruler will spend his time in peace and love.

The daughter turns to the secretary.

"And take this first decree from the new ruler of the Arkonens."

"I, Lucia, as the new ruler of the Arkonens, inform that all hostilities against all peoples and individuals are from this moment lapsed and we will, in cooperation with these, build a world in respect for all life in the light of love, as my name offers me to be."

Copies of the two decrees are written and the former ruler takes the two originals, now signed, from the table and hands them to me.

"I have won my greatest victory today, the victory over my own shadow. Take these and spread the word."

I smile, but do not stretch out my hand to receive the documents. For a moment he seems confused, as if the light he had just experienced was extinguished and he stood alone in the darkness.

"These two documents carry a lot of strength," I say. "They shall remain here in the palace, but I will happily receive two other documents with the same wording from the head of the light."

I turn to Lucia, and she actually lights up as a mighty, pink and golden flame that spreads throughout the room. She hands me two documents with a smile, and at the moment when our eyes meet, I see a connection to lives other than this, and feel the incredible strength that she is now about to manifest in her new realm.

The big Chinese

I am in my living room, the walls of which consist of wooden frames with a net of cross-laid wooden strips covered with light paper. A low elevation that takes up half the space is filled with colourful cushions in a smooth fabric that reflects light. I move between the cushions and step into my moccasins at the edge of the elevation. I have just finished my nap at noon and wash my face and hands.

I am a large and powerfully built man with a smooth head from the forehead up to the top and a plait down the back. I look at my powerful hands; they are well groomed and have a yellowish skin. I feel very comfortable, almost happy. This is a good life. My dark-blue silk kimono with gold embroidery is heard softly when I move across the wooden floor towards the sliding door at the other end of the room. A servant who sits outside slides the door silently to the side and I move out onto a walkway which turns out to be a balcony going all around the room. The balcony is covered, and in the evening, or when the weather requires it, the opening of the balcony to the yard and the garden can be covered by wooden plates to protect my room. I find myself on the first floor, and from up here can look down at the fenced patio. All is in peace. The sun shines and the wind moves the flowers and leaves of trees only slightly. It's a glorious day.

I walk to the right, around the corner, and can now look down into the yard on the other side of the house. The yard is paved, and here is the gate to the outside world. In contrast to the patio's peace, here is a lot of activity. Here are workshops and workspaces of various kinds. Servants, workers and messengers are running back and forth with their countless chores. Most of it takes place in absolute silence. Even the small wagons move quietly across the paving, thanks to the ropes tied around the wooden wheels. It is like standing in the marketplace in the city while putting my hands over my ears. Only guests are allowed to drive into the inner courtyard with the normal, bouncing wheels. Otherwise I do not want to be disturbed by the noise of the wagons and people's clattering clogs.

I stretch and look at the landscape around the building complex. There are fields at all sides interspersed with fruit orchards, low forest vegetation and irrigation channels. The roads wind in all directions through the landscape, among other things to the mill, fish ponds, the workers' huts, the forest in the distance, and to the town and river, of course. Many people move around out there as small coloured dots, doing their own chores to keep all of this machinery going.

"Tea," I say, and a servant shows up with a big cup of steaming tea and a napkin. The tea has an aromatic, lemon-like fragrance and flavour. With my tea cup in one hand and the napkin pinched under my belt, I continue around another corner and see the wall that shields the paved courtyard from the garden. Although I feel at home at the royal court, as in the marketplace and the workshops, it is nature that gives me the greatest satisfaction and tranquillity. This includes the fields, the forests, the fish ponds and the river. But when I must have absolute peace, the best place is my wonderful garden. Here the gardeners move about with their countless chores, which gives me the satisfaction of knowing that something is being created. The sounds of the small streams and waterfalls are soothing, and I can sit and be absorbed by a flower or an insect and feel a cohesion with everything.

After having rounded yet another corner, I go to the stairs leading down to the garden. As I slowly descend one step at a time, I enter a heady scent that encloses and welcomes me. When I step on the stone tiles, the heat hits me, but it is a pleasant heat mixed with the moisture from the water which has just been added to the delicate plants. The evaporating water brings out the smell of soil, and I sense a deep connection with the Earth.

A distinct joy fills me and I think in happy anticipation of the excursion which I will make down to the river shortly. I will have lunch with my beloved Jun on a rug in the shade under the big tree. I know that the tears will run down my cheeks when she sings her mournful and emotional songs. And I know that the cool white wine will make me light headed, and Jun's caresses will awaken the butterflies in my belly. Joy, beauty and love are life's greatest gifts.

A low bench, close to some rippling water, invites me to sit for a short while with my eyes closed and the other senses open before I go back to the daily chores. There is a lot to do, and there are many who wait to talk to me about different errands. I love both the great activity and the calm. Everything in its own time. I take a deep breath and get up. I must move on with my life.

The misdeed

I have come to realise that I do not necessarily appear wiser from one life to a later life in chronological order. I must therefore presume that it is not wisdom as such that has the highest priority in life. I have also wondered if I have been, shall we say, a bad person in other lives. This is confirmed by this small sequence, though it is at the mild end of the scale, even though it is painful for the victims. I am the steward in the dream, but I observe it from a place nearby and am not involved in the person's thoughts, feelings and pain.

Mr Verner, the steward, sits naked on the wooden horse which, for this special occasion, is located in the middle of the dunghill. His hands are tied at the back and his feet below the horse's belly. His pale, white body shines in contrast to his penis covered in dung, which is covered with flies. Is he even alive?

"Mr Verner?" someone is crying. His eyelids slide open a little and there is a twitch at the mouth.

"Cut him down, someone!"

When his tired feet are cut loose, he slides sideways off the wooden horse and ends up in slush with a splash.

"Ugh, how disgusting!"

He has once too often imposed himself on one of the girls. The wrong one, you can say. A girl related to one who had enough balls to do something about it; or at least one whose beaker had run over.

I do not know whether Mr Verner's subsequent condition is due to a mental breakdown, because someone had dared to attack him, or whether it was the blow to the back of the head that he incurred before he, probably unconscious, was tied to the wooden horse; or perhaps it was the time he had spent on it.

Usually a ride on a wooden horse would be more humiliating than painful, but because Mr Verner was not accustomed to suffering this physical and emotional burden, it could, along with the blow to his head, be why he was so vague and confused. It is probably a combination of these things. I know that Mr Verner never became his old self, but toddled about, spoke without any sense and could not harm a fly.

I have received other flashes of doing nasty things where I experience being more directly involved.

For example, in insanity, I felt it necessary to cut a woman I had killed into pieces and put the pieces in small bottles or jars. It was not to get the body out of the way, and I did not have the feeling that anyone knew I had killed her. But I felt a great necessity to treat the corpse in this peculiar way subsequently. I did not receive any explanation as to why it was necessary, but there was perhaps not a reason, only the feeling that it was essential.

It happened in a dark wooden shed, perhaps a workshop. The room was divided into two by a large working table over which shelves hung from the ceiling bearing things that I did not focus on.

This time, which only lasted a few moments, I do not experience the scene in the first person, but can sense the man's feelings while completing the misdeed.

Servant for an Egyptian prince

There is a standstill in the battle. The prince rests on his couch under the tent canvas at the battlefield. The fighting has been fierce, and he is exhausted. He must gather his strength before he can fight again. I have washed him and rubbed him with fragrant oils. He lies on his back with his eyes closed and his arms along his sides. I place myself at his feet and put my hands on his knees. He sighs. I feel the energies flowing through my palms, and the muscles and tendons in the prince's knee joints begin to regenerate. The waste substances loosen up and will be excreted. I give him some more water to drink. He protests. He is too exhausted, but I remind him that it is necessary, both for cleansing and for the fluid balance of the body. He drinks a little water. I call him A-Tara and My Prince, although the ownership is more the other way around.

After the prince has rested, I can finally get him to eat. I have ordered something that is easy to eat and which can also give him strength and energy. Fried bird, bread, fruit pieces soaked in honey, and fruit juices. Finally, a tonic tea.

I feel great devotion to A-Tara. I do not envy his position because the pressure and responsibility are enormous. Through his upbringing, there has rarely been time for pleasures and to relax, or just to do what he has wanted. That is why my goal has been, since I was assigned to him, to make his life as easy and enjoyable as possible. Fortunately, as his personal servant, I have a great influence over the lower-ranking service employees, which makes it easier for me to get a lot of things done.

Stone age

I walk along an ice-covered coast in a large bay and hear the sea roar farther out where the ice stops. It is thaw; the ice is soft and I must move on the beach which is filled with rocks and boulders of all sizes. The ice blocks, huge and small, that mingles with the rocks, bear clear signs of the fact that the higher temperatures of spring are about to take over. The ice in the bay is brash ice, which has been blown here by the wind. The ice uses the night's few degrees of frost to try to stay intact, but its days, as a solid structure, are numbered. A little further in from the beach is a bank with dead grass from last year, but it will quickly change, and spring's vegetation will soon create life and colour here. The bank is partly held together by the roots of the low pine trees. These pine trees form the front of a larger pine forest stretching further into the land.

My clothes are of animal hide, mostly wolf and reindeer, and I have moccasins on my feet. The wolf coat with the hood will be replaced with a shirt of soft hide from a reindeer when it gets a bit warmer, and the long loin cloth, which is now quite ragged after a long winter, will be replaced with a short one that provides better mobility. The next pair of moccasins will be fitted with air vents so the feet do not boil. I am very pleased to sense that the warmth arrives, and I think about the berries and fruits I will munch, but I must wait quite some time. For now, I must settle for the memory of the taste.

I am on a hiking trip, but I am staying for a few days at a nearby hunter-gatherer camp where my belongings are located. I'm travelling alone.

I am brought back from the memories of summer sweetness when I discover a few reindeer that have come down to the beach. They are clearly frightened. First, I reckon it is someone from camp who chases them, but then a pair of wolves emerges. No doubt it is them they are trying to escape from. Now more wolves show up. I look around to make sure that I cannot be surrounded by the wolf pack and discover a man from camp who comes from a different direction and who has also seen the animals. He has his hunting gear, both the spear and the bow. The quiver hangs so low on his back that he can grab an arrow by reaching under the arm that holds the bow. The quiver jumps up and down when he moves. As I am not armed, I naturally assume the role of beater, who chases the animals towards the hunter. I move along some ice blocks when I am discovered by a wolf that acts as a beater, or chaser, for the wolf pack. It must have heard me, for it has already pushed its body against the ground to jump me. I don't think before it attacks me by leaping for my neck. One arm moves up to protect me from the attack. I am not afraid of whatever outcome the match will bring.

As Yadar and observer, I wonder about this, but it must be a natural part of life at the time. Death is there every day, so you would live in constant fear if you hadn't made death a natural part of life.

I manage to keep the wolf's head lifted above mine with one forearm pressed against its neck while I grope for a short-bladed knife that I carry in my pocket. I quickly get the knife out of the sheath and the wolf dies with a howl and then a whine as I stab it in the throat. Under normal circumstances, a wolf will not attack a human being, but its instinct told it that I was a competitor. Or it was merely the ecstasy from the hunting that controlled it. The knife, the blade of which is no longer than my shortest finger and made of stone, I carry as a memento of my father, who made it and gave it to me when I was only a child. I have only a faint memory of my father, but I always carry the knife.

I have gone to my knees and now topple the wolf to the side so I can get back on my feet. The wolves have gotten hold of one reindeer, and, as I turn, I see the hunter releasing the bowstring and hear the sound of the arrow that pierces the heart of the other reindeer which, in its state of panic, has run toward him. With the dead wolf on my back, I run to him, as it is not wise to stay alone near a brought-down prey when there are wolves nearby.

The man is strongly built and with black hair and beard. He has friendly, dark eyes and looks at me with a broad grin.

"You got yourself a hot wolf coat, I see! However, I do not see any weapons. How did you do that?"

"Normally I would take my knife with me, but I only had plans for a short look around the bay. I always have this little thing with me. It's my first knife. I got it from my father when I was quite young."

He turns the little knife in his big fist.

"Yes, a little is better than nothing, but it could easily had gone differently, so that it was the wolf who got himself a pale meal."

He gives back the knife and presents himself.

"I'm Olger and am here with my woman and two kids; well, and a third on the way."

I introduce myself as Jorge.

Olger quickly cuts up the reindeer while I remove the skin of the wolf. I keep the skull as well, but leave the rest. The wolves will take that. Afterwards we help each other to carry the prey back to the camp.

While we struggle back to the camp, I say that I am hiking alone and do not have a family. Olger invites me home. He is in the camp with two of his brothers and their families. He will give me half of the reindeer, as he had not been able to carry the whole thing home alone, and the wolves would probably have claimed the other part before he could have returned for it. However, we made a trade whereby he received the whole reindeer and the wolf hide, and I in turn received a ready-made reindeer hide from last summer. Now I have enough to make my new clothes. The hair side must keep out the spring rain. The hairs on the spring garment will worn off quickly, but I will make summer chothes of the animals fine summer coat.

Finally we are back at the camp, and we throw our loads in front of Olger's tent. A woman sticks her head out of the tent, and then comes out and greets us. The woman is heavy, but Olger lifts her up as if she was a nymph.

"This is Jorge. He has helped me carry the reindeer home. He is a little fellow, but has evidently hidden powers. He also struck a great chap of a wolf, almost with his bare hands."

"My name is Fridun. Do not mind Olger. He does not have great polish, but he speaks right from his heart. Therefore he does not lie, even though he sometimes has a somewhat lively imagination."

Two dirty children come out from the forest. They must have heard their father's voice. Two dogs are with them, which is a good thing when there are wolves nearby.

"Father, father, we have caught a bear," they cry out, while they, with shiny eyes, fling their arms around their father's neck.

"Hmm," Olger says. "I assume it is one of the dead kind, right?"

"Yes, it is more the skeleton, but it has been really dangerous!"

It is the boy who speaks. He is probably six years old, a year older than his sister.

"Who are you?" the girl asks.

"My name is Jorge and I'm travelling out in the big world. I have seen the skeleton of the bear in the forest. It was once a decent bear to hug. What's your name?"

"Stinne," says the girl, and turns a little shy when I come close to her in this manner.

"And I am Bjørn," the boy says. "It's because I am becoming as big and strong as my dad."

His mother rumples his messy hair.

"You probably are, considering all the food you bring in. Soon you'll eat as much as your dad."

"I am hungry," the boy immediately says, now that he is reminded of food.

His mother turns her eyes to the sky and points to some flat stones where there are leftovers from breakfast.

Olger and I first get a cup of water, and then Fridun make a hot tea for us. I pour a bit of cold water into the tea so I can drink it right away. Shortly after, I put down the mug, fetch my hunting knife from my bivouac, and then all three of us start to cut up the reindeer.

The camp site is not in the pine forest, but in a clearing surrounded primarily by deciduous trees with only individual pines. Around the edge of the clearing is a kind of fencing of pine branches and other wood to keep wild animals out. Each family has at least one tipi. Later on, there will be some light huts in which to store their collected food. There will also be smoke-making stoves for fish and meat. The people also need to make a pair of boats. Olger estimates that the site will accommodate a couple more families, but if more arrive they must go further up the coast because this place will not be able to sustain more. Fortunately, one can always visit. Since I do not plan to stay here for long, I have made myself a low bivouac with a bed of pine twigs.

Later in the evening I get the nickname Wolfbane. In my opinion, it was much fuss to make about my killing a wolf with such a small knife, even if it was a great chap. Wolfbane means wolf killer.

Wolfbane

I am in a village with muddy streets. It has been raining and, as people walk around, more and more mud is being worked up. In the middle of the village is a large and muddy space being used as a marketplace. The village has no defences, so when it is rumoured that there are hostile men on the way from the north, the local magnate orders everyone to help build a bulwark of planks as a small fort in the middle of the open space. Everyone works as hard and as fast as they can, and the fort becomes large enough that everyone can seek refuge here. I am part of this work, but I am not from the village and do not live here. My name is once again Wolfbane.

I cannot say that we won the battle. It was probably more that the attackers abandoned their work when they saw the fortifications. They randomly looted the village, but our archers made it difficult for them, and the residents had not left anything of significant value outside the fort. It was not in this village that wealth flourished.

In the evening we celebrate outside. All are gathered between the hills outside the village, and food and drink is laid out on rugs spread over the heather in the hollows. Fires burn here and there, with a smell of fried meat in the air. A boy starts to sing and others follow. It's a song that everyone on the site knows, except me, but I know the boy from somewhere else, another time. The song evolves into a chain dance through the landscape. There is a relieved atmosphere and a sense of unity.

The next day, the village people start building a planked street through the town to stay clear of the mud. The planks come from the fort, now that it has done its job. I am not involved in this work as I walk over the heath towards new experiences.

The Cathar

I sit in an open cart drawn by horses. I am on my way to a meeting to which some of my friends are also invited. It is more that the king has ordered us to come to the hearing about his decision concerning our future in an important matter. I feel a deadly fear and do not reckon that my life will last much longer.

The cart comes to a large, single-storey stone building with a high-pitched roof. A number of soldiers are present. I feel cold, as if it is winter. The door is open and there is a guard on each side. There are more carts, and, besides the soldiers' horses, I recognise some of my friends' horses from their coats of arms. I walk with hesitant steps through the door. There is a soldier on either side of the door inside as well. It is one big room with a few fireplaces that can't possibly warm up the room. Only one is lit, but torches are set up in the retainers on the walls. They are supposed to brighten the room, but for me, in my state of mind, their flickering, yellow light simply means that everything in the room throws scary, dark shadows. There is a long table in the middle of the room and chairs with high backs placed around it. While looking down, I go straight ahead and sit on a chair that is located roughly in the middle of the long side of the table and just opposite the door. We all sit in silence. The only sounds are the occasional rattle of a chair against the stone floor, and otherwise the crackle and popping of fire in the fireplace and the hissing of torches.

The king's envoy has not shown himself yet, but I saw the wagon outside. He must be in the main building. We wait endlessly, but finally there is a stir in the yard and the envoy comes in. He acts to show he is important and is slow to get started. Many documents are read aloud, but the gist is that we must renounce our heretical beliefs, which include rebirth, among other things, as well as promise not to use arms against the king.

Now I see everything through a blur and I feel a terrible fear. Next I experience that I am in the yard and two soldiers hold me down while a third cuts off my right hand, my sword hand.

The secrets of the alchemist

I feel that this chapter, though different in expression, somehow fits in between the previous and the next. It came to me like a flow of information as if I was this alchemist.

Acting as an alchemist is a way to access people with influence and thereby influence them to take a different view. Often, however, people do not have the awareness to receive and understand the so-called secrets of alchemy. You can drag the horse to the water trough, but you cannot force it to drink, as one says.

The alchemist does not convey religion or beliefs, because faith is simply the other side of doubt, which means that faith must continually be confirmed.

Basically, the alchemist does not convey mental knowledge, but a resonance in the individual person's consciousness.

Below are some secrets of alchemy.

You are human and spirit and there is no god above you.

You will not be convicted, punished, or rewarded for your deeds.

You are the creator of your life by the choices you make, and your life is your responsibility.

You, as a soul, are eternal. Because you are eternal, you are not created.

The soul is your consciousness. Wisdom is your soul's experiences through the human, and the human is the tool of the soul through which it experiences.

The soul is your compassion.

The soul is your love and acceptance of yourself.

You have shut out your soul if you don't love yourself.

Meet your soul in the feeling, "I exist!"

Energy has come through consciousness, the soul.

Anything but consciousness is energy.

Energy is personal, cannot be taken from you and there is plenty of it.

Energy is created for you to use.

You don't have to work to get energy. Energy works for you and your deepest commandments.

If your deepest commandments are that you will experience not having enough energy, then the energy will give you that experience.

Time is energy.

Energy can be transformed into neutral or dormant energy and thereby recycled.

A mystery school

I, as Yadar, am the observer in this experience.

I experience living in a kind of closed society. It is a place where I love to be and where I feel safe. We usually treat each other kindly and take care of each other, although some discussions make the waves go high.

I feel very much at home here. This certainly does not happen in my time. Everything is different from what I know, apart from the feeling of being home. People's faces, hairstyles and attire are foreign, and so is the building style. I know I have been here for a long time. I have even helped to build most of the castle and the surrounding buildings. Many of the nearby villagers work here or trade with us.

Some of us are called to the "outcast ceremony". This sounds negative, but is actually the culmination of what we have evolved into. We are a small flock that stands on the stage in front of the podium.

The professor says, among other things, "You have truly become men and women who have been found worthy to be sent out into the great world. This to bring your wisdom to those who are ready to receive it.

"You have been part of this society and contributed to it. Here you have gathered wisdom, unique as it is, and grown into the mature and independent people who now must sow the seed, that you have gathered here, in the outer world.

"It is an honour for me to give each of you the title 'magi', and I know that whatever happens out there, and no matter what you think about it, it will contribute to your wisdom and bring your light to those who are ready to receive it.

"Your seeds are ready, but be aware that it may take some time before they sprout. It will be beyond your control. This is solely the responsibility of the beneficiaries."

We are presented with a fine, crimson scarf by the professor. Now we collect our belongings, which are already packed, and flock to the gate. Anyone who has the opportunity to do so will follow us on the way. Parting is very doleful, with sniffs and tears, and none of us really want to leave the site and the people with whom we have long built close friendships.

The mirror in the cathedral

I stand in front of a giant, white stone building with turrets and spires. I cannot see if it is whitewashed or built from marble. The building is equipped with countless large, curved windows with multi-coloured glass that forms beautiful patterns. In front of me there is a huge two-wing, curved gate of dark wood with carved ornamentation of creeping plants and flowers. The ornamentation is painted in subdued greens and reds. The sunlight is reflected from the white walls and the gate's golden bolts. My breath is taken away by the size and beauty of the building that has a backdrop of sky blue, which seems to give the whole scene further depth.

The two wings of the gate slowly open and I meet a dazzling white light that far surpasses the white walls. I am amazed that it is lighter in there than outside in the sunshine. Perhaps the gate only leads to an open yard?

I enter through the open gate and see that the wall opposite me is a mirror which reflects the shining being that I am. I feel a great love and appreciation for what I am, and take a deep breath and sense that, on the exhalation, I release everything which I thought was a part of me, but has kept me down and subdued my light.

I realise I am in a really large cathedral. I am in the middle of the room with arches under the ceiling held up by huge pillars. Although it is a magnificent experience, I soon feel an urge to move on. I turn towards the gate and leave the cathedral and

the reflection of what I am. I must walk out into
life and continue my journey with this wonderful
experience deep in my heart.

A mirror in depth of darkness

I find myself in a dark cathedral where only a little moonlight comes through small windows high up. It is built primarily of wood and it smells rotten, and I can feel that I walk in mud. I am uncomfortable with the situation and looking for a possible exit. First, I walk to one side to follow the wall and search for a door. Here, small rooms appear, one next to the other. In here it is quite dark, and I feel there is something dark and hideous lurking in the corners. I walk from room to room, but do not walk all the way in, as I can see nothing there and I certainly do not want to feel forward with my hands. After being in several rooms, I feel that as long as I keep away from the total darkness, nothing bad will happen. Just as I do not want to enter the darkness, what is in the darkness does not want to get out of there.

Eventually I have been along one side without finding a way out and am now getting impatient. I look back through the large space that I came from and believe I see a gate at the other end. It was not there before. I rush back and almost fall in the mud on the floor. I reach the other end of the large room, and find a large gate divided into two wings. It does not seem to have been opened for a very long time. There is not an actual handle, but the wings overlap. I push for a while and finally get them aside. The doors are to be pulled towards me and I take hold of one, but then I stop. I do not know whether it is the way out, or a big room that hides something quite awful. After collecting myself, I gently pull one wing. I must use all my strength, but it slowly moves. When a narrow crevice has been created, I stop and peek in. It is pitch dark, and it doesn't feel like a door out to the open. However, no foul smell escapes and I decide to make the opening bigger. Now the crack is big enough for me to go through, but I would rather see both wings fully opened before I walk in. I do not want to risk their suddenly slamming together and leaving me trapped in there. I get both doors all the way open, but I still can't see anything. It is as if there is no light there, or as if the faint light in the room I am standing in can't penetrate it.

I slowly move forward with one arm stretched out. I only take one step when I discover that there is a kind of mirror of dark glass in front of me. I don't know if I can see myself in the mirror and move closer to look in it. Yes, there is a slight contour. I stretch my hand forward and try to touch the mirror with a finger. There is something, but it feels like a rubber membrane that gives in and a indentation is formed on the surface. I press a little harder and the opening gets bigger. Now my hand starts to disappear through the membrane and I become very frightened. Will it engulf me? A thought strikes me: "It is your darkness. Are you afraid of yourself?" Can anyone be afraid of themselves? I suppose you cannot truly, but you may be afraid of your possible actions. "I'll do it," I say to myself. "I'll take the choice and the responsibility."

It is not hard to move forward, but as the surface approaches my face I feel a great deal of anxiety. "Further! Take a deep breath and go through." I take a deep breath, hold it and close my eyes tightly before I take one step that gets me through. I stand still a little while with my eyes closed. Then I let out the air and gently take the first breath through my nose. There is no smell, and I slowly open the eyes. It is completely dark, so I close and open my eyes to be absolutely sure that they are open. They are. Suddenly I feel deeply touched, as if a great love is flowing through me. Here is a being, someone who sends me love, but I still cannot see anything.

"Close your eyes so you don't have to exert yourself trying to see anything. I cannot be seen, only sensed."

I close my eyes and stand in this wonderful feeling of being loved. "Who are you?"

"I am," is the cryptic answer.

"What are you doing here in the darkness?"

"I am," it says again.

I sense a smile, but not as a picture of a smiling mouth, but as a smile that is sensed, felt.

"I am just here. I am not doing anything. I am your soul, I am you, and I am with those things that you, like different people in many lives, have denied in yourself. I am here in unconditional love and with full acceptance of these things."

I exclaim, "These things, which are also me! Yes, of course. Hidden away, denied, despised and hated. Now I understand. I'm in the mirror, and the mirror shows me my dark side; so dark that nothing can be seen. I can only escape completely by going through the mirror and realising that in the darkness I find you, my soul, who lovingly embraces the things which have been pushed away by my human selves."

With this realisation, I feel that I am blown by a fresh wind and I see light through my closed eyelids. I remember another cathedral and a different mirror and open my eyes.

I'm in my bedroom where sunlight flows in and understand that it is late in the morning. It is as if I cannot contain this realisation in my mind. It is as if my brain refuses to deal with the experience, and I understand that it is the mind that makes these condemnations and creates this darkness.

Tira, the most beautiful

This dream experience starts with a volcanic eruption. I am quite close and at eye level with the rim of the crater. The volcano has formed a small island in the sea, and I can faintly see the sun disc through the ash from the volcano. Besides the large crater cone that rises above the sea is a smaller down one side. In addition to the lava, the ash creates great problems even far away. As the volcano finally collapses, a tidal wave is formed that is dangerous to the coast in the distance. The experience happens at a fast pace, and soon the ash disappears. I see the island as a ring of rocks with water inside and a small island in the middle. The ring is broken in two places, so there is access to its interior from the sea. I see a very beautiful city down there, built on the ring and all the way to the edge that goes steeply down towards the sea. There is a small harbour with some boats. I sense the words, "Tira, the most beautiful", the name of the island.

A long time has passed between the volcanic eruption and the next experience when I am in the city. I have just bought a house. It is built of sun-dried claystone with a thick layer of plaster and finally whitewashed, so the rain does not dissolve the claystone. All the woodwork is painted bright blue, and the house is in the same style as all buildings on the island. It doesn't have a large foundation, but it consists of two floors plus the area on the flat roof. The house is located relatively close to the low wall that separates the lot from the road, but there is room for a small tiled space in front of the house where I can sit and observe life while I enjoy a glass of tea, or maybe wine, for example a retsina, whichever I prefer at this time of day. The neighbouring houses are close by and built in the same style. The walls, which mark the neighbouring boundaries, are so low that they serve as symbolic boundaries. They are easily stepped over when you are invited to visit. Behind the house is a little more earth, and here all kinds of herbs are grown for tea and spices, and there is room for some vegetables and low fruit trees: lemon, apple, fig and cherry. At the bottom of the garden I share a large olive tree with my neighbour as it grows at the boundary. There are traces of chickens as the former owner's tenant had some in the garden, but I do not want to keep either birds or animals. They are part of nature and should not drag on their lives in the city to end up as food for humans. If I clear the traces of the hens, I can have some vines, just to eat grapes off the stem.

I have just come in from the street and closed the little light-blue wooden gate, which primarily has to keep dogs out. It is close to noon, and the heat flickers from all the brickwork that is not in the shade. After a few steps I reach the door and enter the darkness and the coolness. Though it is neither particularly dark nor cool in the room. My senses fool me because of the strong light and warmth of the sun that I have just left.

"Hmm." I prepare for a critical review of the house. I look around the front room, which occupies about half of the house downstairs. I see that what the previous owner thinks is ready to live in differs from my point of view. The walls and ceiling must be limed, and the clay floor must be sanded straight and a new layer of light clay applied. This should not spoil my good mood at having this house, and, as I walk up the wooden staircase to the next floor, I can feel that it is my house and that it welcomes me. It seems almost as if I've been here before, it is so homely and recognisable.

My eyes are getting used to the light conditions in the room, which is the same size as the one below, but seems bright and inviting. Two doorways lead into two rooms, each of which is about half the size of the room in front. The walls are located exactly on top of the walls on the ground floor. The two floors are virtually identical, except for the entrance at the ground floor and the location of the staircase up to the roof. The wooden hatch to the roof is closed and, as I push it open to the roof, I feel that it needs to be replaced.

I step out onto the roof and, while I enjoy getting a much better view of the neighbourhood than the one I can get down from the street view, I make a mental note that I must place a small cover over the hatch, either of wood or brick. In this way, the hatch and the entrance will be better protected from the torrential downpours later this year. For now, there is only a small ledge around the hatch to prevent rainwater on the roof from getting into the house. I then decide that the cover should be of bricks, and a face and a name appear. I add it to the inner note.

I look over the city, and although the house is not at the highest, I can still see a bit of the sea reflecting the sun in the thousands of waves dancing on its belly. Without the riches of the sea and its opportunities for transport, we would not have a city out here on this lovely island.

Olympia

It starts with a sense of freedom and joy. I find myself outdoors in a large open space outside the wall around a large temple area. There is a low mountain range in the background. It is warm. The sun shines from a beautiful, cloudless sky, and I can feel a faint wind on my body. As I look down at myself, I see that I am naked and a man. There are other naked men around me, all friends or acquaintances. We are on a sports ground, a stadium, just like those we have here in Alt. We are going to start training runs and are here not least to see how we score in relation to each other. We glisten from the oil that we have lubricated each other with, even if it is only training. Spectators are coaches, mentors, theirs and our own servants, and some others who have found the time to visit. The spectators are on an earth embankment that runs all the way around the pitch. All are men. Women do not have access to either the training or the official games that take place every four years. I am good at running and my self-confidence is high. I am only impatient to get started and show what I can do. We are young, free men. We are not slaves or tied in any similar way.

Later that day I find myself in a temple the roof of which rests on large pillars. It is the largest temple in the area. It is cool and I enjoy this coolness after the warm hours of the training course. I love the silence and the sense of peace that I always have here. I do not give credit to the huge statue in the room for these feelings. To me, the statue is a symbol of power and prosperity more than anything else.

It is quite different to be in the temple of Hera, which I always visit before I leave the site. Here I sense the planet itself, not only as a physical object, but as a being, a consciousness. It is like a basic resonance on which everything is built. Here I feel a peace of mind as if the brain and mind are not important. I am always aware of my breathing and heart rate, and here I feel my heart beating. I do not sense Hera as a representation of the planet, but as a counterweight to this. You can call it air or spirit. I do not feel that Hera is the original name, but it is irrelevant. It is here in the temple where the feeling of freedom and joy is strongest. It's a sense of connection to something I may call home without being able to define it further. I must once again ask myself: "If home is not the planet where is it?"

The death camp

I sense the same energy as at my meeting with Azuru Timu, but the surroundings I find myself in are quite different.

1944. Four characters stand before me. At first, I do not know what they mean, but sense that it is a number. A number for a year. The sum of the digits is nine. An end. In a glimpse I see Yeshua with an oval levitating over his head. Then Yeshua fades away and the oval is there alone. It revolves and becomes a circle. A circular delineation without anything inside. Year Zero. Being 1944 after Yeshua. The circle now repeatedly changes shape between a circle and an oval as if it doubts its own value. The circle disappears.

I feel very sick. I have nausea and am close to vomiting. I feel a great sadness and I weep. There is a dense fog around me. The only thing I see is the mist's grey veil. Then the fog lifts a bit and cold penetrates into each fibre in my body. My boots are tightening, and I look down towards my feet that are ice cold. The boots are black and my pants are grey. Oh, I am a soldier and wearing a grey uniform. Wehrmacht? What does this mean?

I have one hand stretched up to the sky. I look up. I see my cap and, further up, a naked infant, dirty and dead, hangs from my gloved hand. I try, with all my willpower, to close my eyes, but I can't. An unbearable sorrow overwhelms me. It is us, me and my people, who have done this. I feel impotence and excruciating shame and I just want to drift away into oblivion; to die in nothingness where nothing is sensed, and everything is dark. I just want to turn into nothing.

The child becomes an unbearable burden and I lower my arm. The fog has cleared further and I see that I stand in a mass grave with thousands of naked bodies of people of all ages and of both sexes. I feel totally depressed, and the child slips out of my gloved hand. It hits my boot and tumbles over a couple of corpses, after which it falls to rest between a woman's leg as if it tries to leave this world and go back from where it had come.

The fog closes around me. Yeshua fades in, but this time a yellow star made of two overlying triangles floats over his head. It appears to be made of fabric. I hear the word "Jude" spat out in contempt. AZU-RU TIMU! The same energy.

Yeshua and the star fade away. It turns dark around me and a number appears. 1945. The sum of the digits is one, I think. A beginning. I sense hope, but at the same time I sense that this life is soon over and that I am not going to experience the year 1945 after Yeshua.

Now I understand that Yeshua has made such a big impression in mass consciousness that they are counting a new era from his year of birth.

The threads are joined

Yadar's ending statement

The book you now read is written by the man with the threads mentioned in the chapters, *Azuru Timu* and *The Boy with the Mask*. A similar book is written in my time in Alt where I am getting on in years and now spend all my time working with dimensional shifting. We must have all our sensitive research shifted away from mass consciousness. I have completely abandoned the work to recreate a hermaphrodite being, but there are still people working on this.

Dimensions and consciousness

Some research that took place in Atlantis about dimensional shifting, of which Yadar speaks, causes problems in what someone calls the Bermuda Triangle. It has nothing to do with aliens *per se*. Things disappear from our dimension, like the temples of the Tian disappeared from Azuru Timu.

In reality, you cannot divide the world into dimensions. The world is built up of energy that fluctuates at different frequencies and communicates how it should be perceived. The ordinary human consciousness can sense within a limited resonance area or field of consciousness. You can compare it with visible light versus ultraviolet light and infrared light, located outside the sensitivity range of the eye. It is therefore a question of being able to shift the frequency of the energy to which things are built, but retaining the structure of things. At the same time, human consciousness must be shifted accordingly so that it can see and act with things and its own body. It is one thing to be able to manipulate energy, but something quite different to work with consciousness.

Then we come to the threads that join in respect to the soul that has added consciousness and wisdom to this story. You can see threads as human lives, threads in every life as life events, threads in each life as personalities, where the dark ones are mentioned in the chapter, *A Mirror in depth of darkness*. All these billions of billions of fragments assembled into one soup of wisdom that is available as consciousness. Faith is only something you believe, a conviction, while true wisdom, unlike cleverness, is a certainty, but without it being confused with knowledge. The approach to that wisdom is done outside the brain, as wisdom, as has been said, is consciousness. The brain does not handle consciousness, but the brain acts like an aperture, as the small hole in a camera that lets consciousness float out and into your life.

You can get other angles to concepts like consciousness, energy, time, as well as many other things in the series, *The Adventures of Luzi Cane*, written under the pen name, Eriqa Queen.

The End

I hope you have enjoyed the book and ask you to take a moment to make a short review on your favourite retailer website.

Thanks in advance, Erik Istrup.

There is a little more to read on the next pages.

Appendix

Atlantis, myth or history?

Atlantis is, of course, a myth. A very persistent myth because the real events behind the myth lie so deeply in our consciousness that we cannot get rid of it until these events have been redeemed.

The name, Atlantis, has always created associations with doomsday scenarios. The emotions and experiences that arise around the doomsday theme are, to a large extent, similar to the emotions and experiences that existed over the last four to five hundred years before the fall of the last ruler. I write "the fall of the rulers" and not "the fall of Atlantis" as it was the ruler's death that ended the era. Because of the atrocities that had taken place, no one wanted to retain as much as the memory of that time.

There is a legend, a myth in many variants, and then there are the events that are at the root of this, paraphrased in other mythological and fantasy-based stories. Psychic people have also sought answers in the astral realms to the question of Atlantis, and have usually brought back garbled pictures, primarily due to their own filters and interpretations of what they have seen or sensed.

What gives further cause for confusion is that part of Atlantis was actually situated in the astral area between the third and fourth dimension. This is what we call the priesthood today, but they also did science, worked to refine this work and made new discoveries in that direction. In a way, it was their knowledge that prolonged the agony. Had they not worked on this, the ruler would not have been able to appropriate this knowledge and thus prolong his life, and thereby also the oppression of the people.

The kingdom collapsed as all realms do. In this case because of a perverted tyrant who wanted eternal life. The same theme is repeated in countless stories.

The Atlantis era arose as a gradual transition from the Lemuria era. The time of Atlantis was not, therefore, a direct successor to Lemuria, but a branch from it, and the two cultures for a long time had a parallel course, until Lemuria slowly dissolved as a realm and the majority of it sank into the sea, with Hawaii as a remnant. From this derives the story of the kingdom sinking into the sea. At one time there was war between the two factions, accelerating the demise of Lemuria.

The country Alt was really just a loose association of four to five areas, each with its own council without an overall management. The people came from the kingdom Mu, which is now known as Lemuria, which was located in the Pacific region. The people who settled in the Atlantis area were those with the greatest lust for experience, both in terms of exploring new lands and what we today want to call science.

In the beginning, all the people knew the great answers and the dynamics of the universe, but in their eagerness to experience, explore, and create, the knowledge of the original creator of the forces faded into the background. It turned into a very physical creation process.

At one time, attempts were made to find the spark of life in all living things. Many discoveries were made, but eventually it led to a uniformity of the body and brain capacity, and there were eventually blockages into the brain that are still being inherited, generation after generation.

The idea that Atlantis sank into the sea is a vestige of the fact that the majority of Lemuria sank into the sea, as mentioned above. The archipelago, Hawaii, is the remains of Lemuria and, as we know, the islands are created by volcanic activity. When a volcano collapses, it can happen very quickly. A large part of the population managed to escape, but only a few managed to find places to settle. Lemuria sank into the sea long after Atlantis had been founded.

The meaning of the numbers

0 – I am, the individual soul.

1 – Beginning and renewal.

2 – Duality.

3 – Catalyst. The power that gives me access to opportunities based on my instant prerequisites. The number to select. Connects with 5.

4 – Balance, planet Earth.

5 – Change and movement.

6 – Harmony. Balance without duality.

7 – The creative aspect of the universe.

8 – All I have experienced, my wisdom from all lives.

9 – Completion, finalisation. Connects with 1.

11 – Enlightenment, to be able to see. You question the world order and feel that there is more to life. You search for more.

22 – You know you are consciousness.

33 – The old Master energy. The enlightened: The soul leaves the body.

44 – The new Master energy. The enlightened: The soul remains in the body.

Choose a simple living

Yadar learns much about being human and how we are seduced by mass consciousness, our emotions and imaginations. In my book, *Chose a Simple Living*, I describe some of these facts, as well as presenting tools to live a more conscious life that is not filled with drama.

You learn how to become the one who governs your life by becoming aware of the nature of life, thereby getting closer to the concept of free will. The majority of people only use the 'free will' to choose the colour of their shirt, and then they react the rest of the time.

The main character, Yadar

After feeling the name of the book's protagonist, Yadar, I looked for information about the name. I find that it is used as a female name, and I find a description of the properties associated with the name. It actually turns out that the personality of the protagonist I have created fits very well with the description.

> *The name Yadar has created a sympathetic nature with the desire to link friendship and understanding, both socially and in the business world.*

> *The peaceful and disarming appeals to you, and you wish, of course, to have security in a home where your life can follow a certain pattern and where you should not make major decisions.*

You have difficulty in taking specific positions, partly because you lack self-confidence, partly because you do not like issues creating discord between people.

Procrastination is a weakness in your nature that prevents you from completing your plans or concentrating for a long time.

Although the name Yadar creates the urge to understand others, it should be emphasised that it limits your vision and often turns you against technical details.

This name, when combined with a last name, can confuse happiness, satisfaction and success, as well as cause health weaknesses in the liquid and waste system.

Was it the choice of the name that created the person, Yadar, or was it the person whom I had imagined that caused me to choose the name, Yadar? I chose the name very early in the process, but the main character was, after all, in a sense, already created.

About the author

I was born in 1961 in Denmark. I saw my first UFO when I was in 8th grade, in the middle of the day, during a playtime.

I started to write in my early years, but it was not until I saw the possibility of self-publishing that I created books.

I am a qualified technical artist, technical assistant and electronics engineer. I completed my latest work as a technician in 2005 and got a bachelor's degree in social education in 2010.

In 2003 I started at healer education, mostly after working hours, and completed part 1 in 2005. This was one of the major steps towards a more metaphysical approach to life. During that period, I came in touch with several people who are media for non-physical beings, which gave me further insight. Gradually, I grew more confident in my own skills and could eventually sense the information that benefited me in everyday life.

In 2011 I went to Greenland for my first work as a social educator, working with people with autism spectrum disorders until October 2017. I went to Denmark and gradually started to work as a writer and publisher.

Erik Istrup, Danmark, January 2019

www.ingramcontent.com/pod-product-compliance
Lightning Source LLC
Chambersburg PA
CBHW020114310726
48970CB00002B/627